TORONTO SOUND

VOLUME 1

A MEMOIR OF THE CITY'S RISING PRODUCERS

Produced by KLFTN

SOUND SUPREMACY
ENTERTAINMENT

Copyright © 2016
Sound Supremacy Entertainment, Inc.
(info@soundsupremacy.com)

All rights reserved. No part of this book may be reproduced in any form or by any electronic or mechanical means including information storage and retrieval systems, without permission in writing from the author. The only exception is by a reviewer, who may quote short excerpts in a review.

ISBN: 978-0-9952605-0-4

First Edition

Printed in Canada by Marquis Printing
Editor and Cover Concept: Sibyl Creative Consulting
(sibylcreative@yahoo.com)
Cover Design: Lance Comrie/weSEWsick (wesewsick.ca)
Interior Layout: Julie Hodgins (www.juliekaren.com)

Visit our website: www.battleofthebeatmakers.com

FOREWORD

Music gives melody to our greatest hopes and aspirations. It adds harmony to the days of our years. It is the unfolding of the soul's song, and the paint that gives color and vibrance to the canvas of our lives.

Hip-Hop music has become one of the wonders of the modern world. Its most celebrated method of expression has been through rapping, which is the vocation of the emcee. Rap music, which is the younger sister of Jamaican dancehall, is all about ridding the beat with impeccable cadence, confidence, and cleverness.

While it can certainly be argued that The Last Poets, or even Muhammad Ali, contributed to the Hip-Hop music aesthetic, rap in its modern context, is an art form with roots in the Bronx, New York. Its Father is

DJ Kool Herc from Trench Town, Jamaica. Since revving up partygoers on Sedgwick Avenue in the Bronx in the 1970s, Hip-Hop music has become the very foundation of pop culture which is the United States of America's most lucrative global export.

After turning the New York City night scene on its ear, Hip-Hop music and culture spread to the West Coast, the Dirty South, and all places in between, eventually taking the world by storm. But what about Canada?

Drake, who has had the highest-selling rap album of 2016 thus far with *Views*, is undoubtedly the world's most recognized rapper representing Canada today. This has opened new doors of opportunity for up-and-coming artists—who in the eyes of many Americans—hail from a country that is still more recognized as the home of Bret "The Hitman" Hart than it is for Hip-Hop hit men who've bodied Billboard's rap charts.

This is why KLFTN's ground-breaking memoir, **Toronto Sound**, is such a critically groundbreaking literary contribution for those of who treasure the storied history and culture of Hip-Hop as a global phenomenon.

As a cultural ambassador of Canadian Hip-Hop, KLFTN details the role that his famous Battle of the Beat Makers competition played in assisting in the development of careers of familiar artists like Drake, Boi-1da, and T-Minus, while exposing us to a litany of other rappers and producers who have helped to establish Toronto's Hip-Hop scene over the course of nearly three decades.

A devoted father, and a persistent business man, Reddick takes us on a journey to Northern parts unknown to highlight the true grit and the grind, behind Toronto's beats and rhymes. Without any further ado, the Canadian crowner of the beat makers brings to you, the gift of **Toronto Sound**.

Adika Butler

TORONTO SOUND

VOLUME 1

TABLE OF CONTENTS

CHAPTER 1 — 9
THE JOURNEY BEGINS

CHAPTER 2 — 29
BATTLE OF THE BEAT MAKERS I
(BBM I - MARCH 2005)

CHAPTER 3 — 51
BATTLE OF THE BEAT MAKERS II
(BBM II - MAY 2005)

CHAPTER 4 — 67
BATTLE OF THE BEAT MAKERS III
(BBM III – AUGUST 2005)

CHAPTER 5 — 85
BATTLE OF THE BEAT MAKERS IV
(BBM IV – MARCH 2006)

CHAPTER 6 — 101
BATTLE OF THE BEAT MAKERS V
(BBM V – AUGUST 2007)

CHAPTER 7 — 117
BATTLE OF THE BEAT MAKERS VI
(BBM VI – AUGUST 2008)

A MEMOIR OF THE CITY'S RISING PRODUCERS

CHAPTER 1

THE JOURNEY BEGINS

Upon my arrival I was greeted by the sounds of Earth Wind & Fire, The Jackson 5, The Manhattans, The O'Jays, James Brown, The Commodores, Kool & The Gang, The Gap Band, McFadden & Whitehead, Smokey Robinson, Al Green and a long list of others which consisted of Funk, Soul, Disco, Gospel, R&B, Rock, and even Country.

This journey began on September 24th, 1975, in a small town called New Glasgow, Nova Scotia. Born to a Black (Indigenous) Nova Scotian woman and Central African man in a tight-knit community known as The Vale Road. It was here that I experienced the sounds that would shape my musical taste buds for years to come. Temporarily residing with my grandparents, and being surrounded by a host of other relatives, instilled a strong sense of family and belonging. This was the essence of what we call "Down Home". The Vale Road was a predominantly Black (Indigenous) community, consisting of people who have resided in the province of Nova Scotia for well over 200 years.

I left the Vale Road in 1981, and landed in the west end of Toronto in a building fondly referred to as "The Brown Building" at 3390 Keele Street, near Sheppard Avenue West. My neighborhood was a melting pot of cultures consisting of African, Caribbean, Southeast Asian, Chinese, Middle Eastern, European, South

American and those who would just prefer to consider themselves Canadian.

Many, if not most, were first generation Canadians. But none of this mattered to my childhood peers. We occupied our time only concerned with games like marbles, kick-the-can, chase, baseball, basketball, playing on monkey bars, wrestling, slap-boxing, and a litany of mischievous activities that would help us become who we were meant to be. Somewhere in the middle of all of this, we were often enchanted by the sounds of Michael Jackson, Prince, Madonna, Eddy Grant, Musical Youth, Rita Marley, Bob Marley & The Wailers, Dennis Brown, and whatever else captured our imaginations from the world of pop culture. Oftentimes we just heard our parents playing what would range from funk, disco, soul and R&B to calypso, soca, reggae and eventually dancehall. Music was always around, and we were often dancing but, it was more or less a happenstance activity.

WILD STYLE

This changed dramatically between '83 and '86. In this period, three classic movies dropped: Wild Style ('83), Beat Street ('84) and Breakin' ('84), which would alter our worldviews forever. This all was accompanied by a sound that captivated our minds, bodies and souls. This sound was created by the likes of Chief Rocker Busy Bee, Double Trouble, The Cold

Crush Brothers, Coke La Rock, Afrika Bambaataa and the Soul Sonic Force, and many others, including Kool Herc, who I would learn about in later years.

Breakdancin' had us in a trance. No longer were we randomly dancing to our parents' music, we found something that we connected with directly. As a result, we spent countless hours practicing, performing and battlin'. The tick, worm, windmill, tuff windmill, shufflin, handspin, backspin, fleur, uprockin, crab, and if you were brave enough, the headspin. The worm was my particular trademark move. Older heads use to argue with one another trying to take credit for teaching me.

There were countless songs that we loved to breakdance too but, some of the standout songs included: Malcolm McLaren's "Buffalo Gals", Herbie Hancock's "Rockit", Art of Noise's "Beat Box", "Shannon's "Let the Music Play" and Joeski Love's "Pee Wee's Dance." Still, I would have to say that Newcleus' "Jam On It" took the cake. During the mid-80s, this song had the same inspiring effect on me that Mobb Deep's "Shook Ones Pt. 2" had during the mid-90s. Different vibrations but, similar effect, one inspired you to breakdance and another inspired you to spit bars. Yet both were expressions of the same cultural force.

Somehow I often found myself in between two age groups: the older heads, who were already knee-deep in all the latest trends, music, and cultural innovations and the younger heads who spent a lot of time playing Atari or Nintendo, watching Transformers or He-Man, playing Knicky-Knicky 9 Door (bangin' on random apartment doors and running) to have fun. This younger crew would grow up to be known around Toronto as the DJ crew, "The Ill Kidz".

FANTASTIC VOYAGE

It was during this time, in the mid-80s, that I somehow stumbled onto a radio program called *The Fantastic Voyage Program*, hosted by Ron Nelson. The show aired every Saturday from 1pm-4pm (on CKLN 88.1 FM) which became a highly coveted timeslot for well over a decade, as succeeding hosts seamlessly continued the legacy. Without a doubt, he is the architect behind spreading Hip-Hop throughout Toronto during the early to mid-80s.

I would personally consider him the Kool Herc of Toronto. About 85% of the Hip-Hop I heard or had access too came from listening religiously to his show. Cassette tapes, a walkman and/or a ghetto blaster were the order of the day. My peers and I would record his show onto cassettes and that was our fix until the next show, the following week. Another 10% came from borrowing friends' cassettes. Those with a good enough reception, got there music from WBLK in Buffalo, New York. Some who travelled to New York City would bring back all the latest music from Mr. Magic or DJ Red Alert's radio shows. The final 5% came from my Mom buying me albums like Grandmaster Flash and the Furious Five "The Message" ; UTFO "UTFO"; Fat Boys "Fat Boys"; Run DMC "RUN-D.M.C.", "King of Rock" and "Raising Hell"; Whodini "Escape"; Beastie Boys "License to Ill" and LL Cool J's "Radio".

The drums used on LL Cool J's song "Radio" would leave such an impression on me that it would be the deciding factor in me inviting Drake, via Boi-1da, to perform one of his first songs "Do What You Do." Nearly 20 years after the Kangol King from Queens dropped the Hip-Hop classic, Drake had his debut rap performance at Battle of the Beat Makers IV in 2006. More on that later.

In 1987, I was bombarded with several distinct artists and groups that would totally change the game, ushering in what some dubbed The First Golden Age in Hip-Hop. Boogie Down Productions (BDP), Public Enemy, Big Daddy Kane, Eric B & Rakim, Biz Markie, Kool G Rap, EPMD, Slick Rick, X Clan, Brand Nubian, MC Lyte, Queen Latifah, Roxanne Shante, Just Ice, Heavy D, Audio Two, Stetsasonic, and many others were all leading the new wave of Hip-Hop, picking up where the earlier school left off.

During this time, Toronto had two legendary spots that you would have to attend if you wanted to experience this thing called Hip-Hop: the Concert Hall (now known as the Masonic Temple at 888 Yonge Street) and Party Centre on 167 Church Street. These two spots would be Toronto's equivalent to the Apollo Theatre or Latin Quarters. There were other venues that popped up but, these two are Hip-Hop landmarks in Toronto.

I attended my first jam in '88 at the Party Centre, having just returned fresh from a bus trip to Buffalo, as was the norm in that day. If you wanted to not only get fresh but, rock something that nobody around the way had, taking bus trips to Buffalo was the thing to do. Some would take bus trips to Flatbush (Brooklyn) for the same effect. It was here that I would see one of my favorite local Toronto rap groups, which I would often hear on the Fantastic Voyage show. Little Rascals from Flemingdon Park. They are not to be confused with the Rascals from Vancouver.

JANE STREET

I moved to Jane Street around 1986-87. Jane Street and Lawrence Avenue West to be exact. I was still attending Elia Jr. High, near Jane & Finch, when another radio station came on the airwaves, just up the street from our school, at York University. CHRY 105.5 FM was born. They came to our school and gave everybody these bright green CHRY pins to promote the radio station. I recall one of the more popular shows on the station having a "pump it or dump it" contest where local artists would get to battle over the airwaves track for track

There is only one artist from this era that stuck in my mind. I believe he went by the name of "JD the waterskiing beatbox" or something to that effect. I used to listen intently to these battles, observing how the production always seemed to lack something, like an ingredient that was missing. Much like how reggae produced in Toronto never quite had the authentic sound that reggae produced in Jamaica had. New York had always been the measuring stick for Hip-Hop production, up to that point, so I was often disappointed with the production I heard coming from Toronto. However, I would be surprised to learn much later that a producer who moved to New York from Toronto, named Mantronix, might have been the originator of the Trap sound that would later come to reign supreme in the Hip-Hop world. Check out a song he produced in '85 for a New York Artist named T La Rock, the song was called "Bass Machine", and you tell me if the rolling high hats, rolling snares and bass sound familiar.

After Ron Nelson stepped down from CKLN and moved deeper into the Dancehall world, with the Reggaemania show, this void was filled by the likes of DJ X, later joined by Michee Mee, a pioneering female Emcee. The Powermove show kept the legendary Saturday 1pm-4pm timeslot rockin'. Others would follow suit such as DJ P Plus and many others. Another station and show would also launch that contributed to pumpin' Hip-Hop in the city, at CIUT 89.5 FM, hosted by Big Brother John Browski and MC Motion. This station would later play a critical role in the legacy of Battle of the Beat Makers.

Years later, I served as a volunteer that would travel up and down Jane Street trying to gain support with a petition form, trying to get a license for a Black owned commercial FM Station, spearheaded by Milestone Communications, which ran from a small office on St. Clair West. Denham Jolly, a Jamaican businessman, ran this operation and a few years later they would make history with FLOW 93.5 FM, coming on the airwaves. There was a lot of high hopes for this station. It is debatable whether they lived up to the expectations. However, as one of the foot soldiers during its early stages, it planted the seed in my mind, that a small grassroots operation could effect change on a larger scale.

TORONTO CLASSICS (PRE-2005)

My Top 3 favorite Toronto Tracks:
1: **Where I'm From** (Black I),
Tie for #2 **Thin Line** (Point Blank) & **EZ on the Motion** (Ghetto Concept)

Some of my additional favorites:

Outsiders (Point Blank & Ghetto Concept)

Boiling Point (Concrete Mob)

Eh Yo (JB)

God Only Knows, Born & Raised In The Ghetto & Thin Line (Point Blank)

Doin It & Pull Up (Rochester)

When I Went to Buy Milk (Base Poet)

Dialtone (Tona)

East Meets West (Aristo & Young Tony)

Elements of Style, On Da Mic & Jamaican Funk (Michee Mee)

My Definition of a Boombastic Jazz Style, Wash Your Face In My Sink, Ludi & Roll of the 12 Sided Dice (Dream Warriors)

Let Your Backbone Slide, Drop The Needle & Conducting Thangs (Maestro Fresh Wes)

VIPs Only (Maestro Fresh Wes & K-4ce)

Boom Craze (Slinky Dee)

Father Time & Hate Runs Deep (Saukrates)

Can't Stop Us & Hip-Hop Don't Stop (Split Personality)

Get Down On Your Knees & I Know Myself (Godd Bodies)

Big & The Throwback (Brassmunk)

T.Dot Anthem & T.R.A.C.K.S Lament 1.5 (IRS)

Ice Breaker (Brasstacks)

Toe to Toe Remix (Nefarius)

Gotta Get Mine (Infinite)

Whose Talking Weight (Redlife)

Pimp Of The Microphone (HDV)

I Rhyme the World in 80 Days (Kish)

EZ on The Motion & Certified (Ghetto Concept)

Rise Like The Sun (K-os)

Informer & Anything For You (Snow)

When You're Hot You're Hot, Money Can't Buy Me Happiness & The Hood is Here Remix (Jelleestone - Jugganaut, Imperial, Stump, JB, Mayhem Morearty, V'Diablo, Payback)

B-Boy Destruction (Ron Nelson)

Natty Dread & Firestarter Album (Kardinal)

Set It Off Remix (Kardinal)

Rage (Thrust)

Ready for the Money (Junior D)

Breakin Atoms Album (Main Source)

Can I Get A Yo, Bubblegum & The Staff (Graphidi Logic)

Brown Bricks (Jugganaut/Frankie Payne)

Structure Foundation, Black Rain, Elements Of Mind & Soldier Story (Citizen Kane)

I Kick Da Flava & Givin Ya A Taste (Apples & Oranges)

A MEMOIR OF THE CITY'S RISING PRODUCERS

ChiLatchiLu (Freaks of Nature)

One By One (Sean Boothe)

Dear Hip-Hop (Dan E O)

45th Dumpin & Jane N Finchin (Smugglaz)

What Goes Around & I'm From Finch (Corey Fila)

I'm From Jane Remix
(Sling Dadz, Blacus Ninjah, Frankie Payne, K Fresh, Smugglaz, Page)

Twenty One Years, Let's Ride & Back Where I've Stayed (Choclair)

Northern Touch (Canadian Posse Cut)

Black Man Wagon & Crazy Jam (Rumble & Strong)

Rest In Power Redway and King Reign.

FOUNDATION PRODUCERS (PRE-2005)

A few of the Producers and/or Engineers that have contributed to the foundational stages of the sound of Toronto include: Mantronix, Slinky Dee, Beat Factory, Dream Warriors, Krush and Skad, Maximum 60, Ron Nelson, Top Secret, The Grassroots, Mr. Attic, Swiff La Roc, Frankenstein, First Offense, DRK, Scam, K-Cut, ERF, K-4CE, Gadget, 2Rude, Pikihed, Blast, Tone Mason, Black Kat, Agile, Sproxx, Saukrates, Solitair, Tara Chase and Kardinal.

It should be noted that during the early stages, for the most part, the music was created completely out of love for the art form. There was no idea that careers would be made from it or that any significant amount of money could be generated from it. That was not really the focus. It was about a feeling, a vibe. The only ambition was to showcase the hidden genius within us that naturally desires to create. Successful records or careers evolved only as a side effect of this passion to create beats and music that just felt good to the soul. However, when it did come down to the business side of it, Canadian labels didn't really believe Canadian Hip-Hop was marketable, not until Canadian artists went south of the border and became successful, or until Americans took what we had and ran with it. Then the labels would pay attention with the exception of Beat Factory.

Pretty much as long as I been listening to CKLN 88.1 FM since the mid-80s, Beat Factory was probably the first and most popular name I would often hear about as a pioneering production team out of Toronto. Responsible for the success of a lot of early Toronto artists like Michee Mee, Dream Warriors, Keshia Chante, Tom Green, Glenn Lewis and several others.

BEFORE YOUTUBE

It is always interesting talking to people nowadays who have grown up in the BET and/or YouTube age, where they can watch music videos 24/7. They can hardly imagine a time when all we got was 5-6 videos a WEEK. Much Music's Rap City (Toronto), which is not to be confused with BET's Rap City (we didn't get that until many years later) provided us with our weekly 30-minute visual dosage of all the music we loved. We would either run home from school or cut our outside activities short, just so we could see a Leaders Of The New School, Biggie, Onyx, or Buju Banton video. Other than going to a live concert or getting a copy of a VHS tape filled with videos, this was our main fix through the 80s and 90s. This would expand in later years, where we would eventually get one hour per week, up until now where we can access music videos 24/7 videos.

Soul In The City was another earlier show that didn't zero in on Hip-Hop but would sprinkle some Hip-Hop flavored music in their show.

Xtendamix provided us with a mix of Hip-Hop and reggae/dancehall videos throughout the 90s, to balance our love for both closely related genres.

Michael Williams and Master T were hosts that provided us with views into the broader music world.

BET would later enter Canada and thoroughly impress the minds of Toronto Hip-Hop heads with whatever the programmers wanted us and the rest of the world to see. We were embellished with the bling culture and sound. From Jay-Z, Rocafella, Bad Boy, Ja Rule, 50 Cent, G Unit, Eminem, Cash Money, No Limit, Death Row, Aftermath, Rap-A-Lot, Dipset, State Property, Ruff Ryders and the eventual takeover of the Dirty South.

BEFORE THE 6IX

The first high school I attended was Weston Collegiate Institute in '88. From going to school with Dayo Ade a.k.a. "BLT" from the Degrassi Junior High series, as well as hood legends like Bill/Rage Elite (RIP), to attending talent shows, where I would see Dream Warriors (first Toronto Hip-Hop group to reach international heights back in '91) perform live before they blew up. I also saw Michee Mee, who had songs buzzin' on the radio like "On Da Mic" and "Elements Of Style", which featured KRS-One (BDP). Jane Street has always been rich in talent and set a foundation for much of my early development in the hip-hop world. I luckily had an opportunity to witness and soak up a lot of this early movement, which would assist me greatly when it was my time to show and prove.

I would later come to learn that the whole city was bringing something to the table. Sound systems, rappers, breakdancers, beatboxers, DJs and producers were coming from every corner of the city and surrounding areas. Jane & Finch, Brampton, Jungle, Mississauga, Regent Park, Malton, Flemingdon Park, Ajax, Mount Olive, Glendower, Doomstown, Vaughan & Oakwood, Esplanade, McCowan & 401, Chester Lea, East Mall, West Mall, Sparroways, Tandridge, Cataraqui, Willowridge, Markham & Eglinton, Village, Orton Park,

Chalkfarm, Galloway, Falstaff, Malvern, Trethewey, Bay Mills, Don Mills, Woolner, Parkdale, Thornhill, Vaughan, Richmond Hill, Pickering and Hamilton were all participating and contributing to the rich foundation of the collective sound of Toronto.

Ron Nelson and Chic Dynasty were key figures that introduced me to the live aspect of a Hip-Hop show during the late 80s and 90s. Shows like "The Monster Jam" was the first and most influential series and would provide me with the building blocks I needed to develop concepts of my own. Equally important were the dancehall Soundclash Culture, Turntablist DJ Battles (Metro Mixoffs, etc) and the DMC DJ Battles. There were a number of shows in the city that ended up turning into a series but, Monster Jam highlighted the battle culture, whether it was for Breakdancers, DJs, MCs or Beatboxers. Most of the jams consisted of artists from Toronto, Montreal, Philly and New York.

Dancehall also played a key role that definitely influenced the forming of Battle of the Beat Makers. From growing up listening to cassette tapes of Silverhawk, Kilimanjaro, Metro Media, King Addies, Bass Odyssey, Earth Ruler, Bodyguard, Inner City, David Rodigan and the foundation sounds of Studio One, to attending actual sound clashes in Toronto or just going to a show to hear Stone Love juggle (playing music without the intent to clash another sound). In Toronto, there was a long list of sound systems right in my backyard, such as Powerhouse, Ghetto Khan, Syndicate, Military, Black Supreme, Black Reaction, Radication, King Stur Grav, King Vower, Black Star, right up to the newer sounds like Rebel Tone and Rootsman. These sound systems all came from various parts of the west end, although there was no shortage of sounds from the east end as well. So the influence of dancehall and Sound Clash Culture is embedded in the fabric of Toronto.

The first documented beat battle in Toronto history took place in 1993, as part of "The Ultimate Hip-Hop Battle", organized by Ron Nelson, which took place at The Opera House, featuring an MC Battle, DJ Battle, Dancer Battle and Producer Battle (with 16 Producers). Some of the names of the foundational producers that participated include: DJ X, LA Luv, First Offence, Alex G, Power, 2Rude, Tyson, Tyjam, S-Blank, Cougar, Blast, Kwame and Born Swift, I could not confirm the other 3 producers.

There is no direct connection between this monumental battle and Battle of the Beat Makers, as I would not come to be aware of this event until nearly 22 years after the fact.

HIGH SCHOOL BLUES

I was in Grade 10 at Northview Secondary School, the first time I shared my future plans in an open setting. I believe it was a Math class or something and I might have been the only black guy in the room. Somehow the teacher got around to asking everybody what they wanted to be when they grew up. I can't recall much of what everybody else said, because I was so focused on what the response would be when my turn came around.

So, eventually my turn comes around and in my opinion I was being totally honest and sincere in my aspirations but, for some reason most of the class, teacher included, seemed to find humor in my goals. I said I was going to start a record label, make music, sell music, shoot videos, you know…run an entertainment company. I honestly didn't think it was too big of a deal to have such goals but, the snickering and amusement that spread around the class had me second guessing.

I was never one to really share my goals with people, much less in a public setting but, I wasn't in the mood to make up some random bullshit. So, I spoke and that short discussion left me with one of my most memorable situations in high school, learning first hand that not everybody will support or believe in your goals, not even teachers.

Technology has changed a lot since those days. When I made those goals we were still dealing with cassette tapes and vinyl; there were no CDs, DVDs, much less an mp3, internet, email and laptops. It would have taken a lot of cash money to fulfill my goals in the time period that I had envisioned them. But, in the future, the changes in technology would cause the cost of production to drop dramatically, making my goals all that much more attainable. Funny how the universe works.

Through Battle of the Beat Makers, I would create a vehicle that would provide me with the opportunity to fulfill all these goals that I had envisioned over a decade earlier, all in one shot. I never shared that experience I had back in Grade 10 with anybody outside of that class. But, it left such a stain in my memory banks. It was a moment of awkward joy the day I paused and realized that I had actually fulfilled all those high school dreams. As we move forward in "time" the advances in technology will continue to make your today goals that much more attainable in the near "future".

PRIVATE SCHOOL CLUES

After becoming disillusioned during a brief stint at George Brown College, studying Mechanical Engineering, I eventually stumbled on a private school that I thought spoke more of my language. This school was Trebas Institute. I started sometime around 1996.

I only remember two of the instructors of the time, one being the owner of Rammit Records, Trevor Shelton, and another being Gadget. He didn't speak much but his presence was always felt. His engineering skills were behind quite a bit of the early Hip-Hop music coming out of Toronto and would carry on into the future. I recall seeing Saukrates for the first time hopping off the bus at Parliament & Dundas, making his way down to Trebas. I suspected he was off to see Gadget.

I was taking an Audio Engineering program during my time at Trebas but, I wasn't totally impressed with the curriculum. Trevor was cool but, Gadget seemed like the only Instructor I could really relate too. I had a gut feeling I could get all the knowledge I needed as an engineer from him but, our class seemed to spend the least amount of time with him.

The other instructors all came from different worlds, which seemed more focused on the technical nature of music, as opposed to the natural ear and sense of creation that most producers I would come to know were driven by. We might not know what a "C Sharp" or "B Flat" was but, that wouldn't stop us from selling a million records or winning a Grammy. There is a hidden genius that exists beyond books or instruction, that's the genius I was interested in, and as a result, my time at Trebas, although informative, didn't offer me the best lessons.

CHAPTER 2

BATTLE OF THE BEAT MAKERS I

(BBM I)

TORONTO SOUND

BACK IN THE T DOT

Having left Toronto in 1997, I returned in late 2002 after spending five years living in Nova Scotia. My leave was spurred by the bullshit that was running rampant in Jane & Finch; from hood wars, to jail, to deportation, to early graves and a whole bunch of other vices and traps set up all around me at the time. Around '96-'97, the Bloods & Crips phenomenon made its way to Toronto and my hood was dead smack in the thick of it. One hood divided by two colors. Unexpectedly, an opportunity presented itself that would lead to me taking a break from the hood and visiting Nova Scotia for a 2-week period.

As fate would have it, this 2-week trip turned into a 5-year journey. I had to let off two burners to get the funds to take this trip. I landed back in Nova Scotia basically broke and quickly found myself on welfare before landing an entry level job in the social services industry. After several years of working I was offered an opportunity to attend Saint Mary's University, free of charge, in a Community Economic Development diploma program. It was around this time that I began to host a show on the local campus station CKDU 88.1 FM.

Different city, but 88.1 FM always had a nice ring to it. One of my childhood dreams manifested with this radio hosting gig. I started off doing the graveyard shift, which were the rites of passage that all new hosts had to go through. Luckily, the graveyard shift was the norm for me. I use to risk my freedom every night on the graveyard shift in Jane & Finch, so this was a cakewalk. After a couple months, I pitched a show to the board called the "Youth Entrepreneurship Show," which was a weekly show that would consist of me interviewing entrepreneurs from all over Canada and discuss their various ventures, while also providing a platform for young entrepreneurs to gain free exposure for their businesses.

I used Saukrates' "Father Time" instrumental as the background theme music for the show. One of my favorite interviewees was Sol Guy, manager of the rap group, The Rascals, from Vancouver, as he provided me and the listeners with a lot of information on the inner workings of the music business. After about a year on the airwaves I ended up winning an award for Local Talent Development from the National Campus and Community Radio Association. Through a friend, Raymond, I later ended up becoming an Interim Station Coordinator at the radio station, while they sought a Director for the vacant position.

While in this temporary role I happened to stumble on a CD that would stop me in my tracks. Listening to this

CD instantly brought me back to the world I temporarily left behind in Jane & Finch. The CD was titled "Everything Happens for a Reason," and the artist went by the name of Jugganot. He represented a section of Jane Street known as Falstaff a.k.a. Brown Bricks, this was also the place I would catch my first case back in '88. From beginning to end, this MC spoke the language of the **Toronto** I grew up in. This was a very accurate depiction of what Toronto sounded like to me. Jane Street produced a lot of talented artists but, unfortunately not many survived to complete a full album.

TRY A TING...

Back in Toronto after 5 years, I felt like someone fresh out of jail, hungry to get something happening. Skilled with the ability to quickly identify resources, programs, and services, I enrolled in a 6-month youth program to get back on my feet. During this time, I reconnected with a cousin of mine, Curtis James, a talented fashion designer who also had an interest in the music business. We spent weeks and months trying to come up with a marketing idea that would help artists sell CDs and also help ourselves in the process. We endeavored to manufacture a machine that was similar to a small CD player with headphones, welded on top of a stand that we would distribute all over Ontario and as people came into their local record shops, barbershops and such, they would be able to listen to a selected artist, based on whichever label we partnered with, to market and distribute their music. It would have been on a small scale to start but, when you're in the idea-generating stage, no idea is too outlandish as far as I'm concerned.

In essence, we were trying to start a distribution company of sorts. However, as newer technology was constantly entering the market we didn't get far. But, we did have a group in mind that we were really interested in pushing with this idea of ours. That group was Point Blank. Representing the first and largest hood in Canada, Regent Park, they became my favorite local group at the time. They had spent years building up a solid street buzz and by the time they dropped their "Top Shottas" mixtape, they were pretty much untouchable. We reached out to members of the group, Imperial (MC) and Pikihed (Producer) and told them we had a marketing plan that could help their situation, as they were in the process of trying to secure a deal. We didn't wanna feed them false promises, because we definitely believed in their music. But, our marketing and distribution plans didn't work quite the way we thought they would.

We settled for distributing their mixtape across Southern Ontario, in places like London, Kitchener-Waterloo, Hamilton, Niagara Falls, St. Catherines, Burlington and within the Greater Toronto Area. We would buy the mixtapes cash upfront from Imperial or Pikihed and then sell it for more to the individual Mom and Pop shops. We spent the summer of 2003 doing this before realizing that for all the gas we were burning driving around the province, this was going to be a short lived experience. However, it felt good to be back in the groove of things, moving, shaking and trying to make something happen.

I also learned a lot visiting all the local campus stations, record shops, barbershops and other local community outlets. It became apparent that no matter where I went in the province, they all looked to Toronto to lead the way. To some, this may seem obvious, but for those kids stuck in the hood all day, they don't understand the power they have by simply living and surviving in Toronto. The whole world gets their cues from what goes on in the hood. Whether that hood is in Compton, Brooklyn, Ninth Ward or in our case, a Regent Park, Rexdale or Jane & Finch.

Even the skeptics I would encounter living in the outskirts of the city were curious to sit down and pick my brain to see what magic was about to come out of Toronto. I didn't know in specific terms but, I had a gut feeling something was about to happen.

A SEED IS PLANTED

As summer of '03 came to an end, a physical seed was planted. This seed was my daughter Kenya. When she was born another seed was planted. However, this one was a mental seed. It would be the blueprint for what would become known as Battle of the Beat Makers (BBM). I had come up with a company name, something strong that would stand out. Sound Supremacy Entertainment. I had several industry people either ask, or suggest, that I change the name for the fact that the word "supremacy" had a negative connotation. I wasn't changing shit. It was final, Sound Supremacy Entertainment was the company and the flagship event would be called Battle of the Beat Makers.

Based on the fact that at the time, there were events that catered to rappers, singers, dancers, poets and DJs. There was nothing that catered to producers. I was never really one to ride a bandwagon, as the Hip-Hop world I grew up in didn't approve of that. I had to find my own lane and carve my own niche. So I decided to jump in the Producer arena to see what would happen. I was aware that beat battles existed in the US, but at the time no such thing existed in Toronto. I was inspired by US beat battles, which I believe were run at the time by a group called the International Producer Association.

Other sources of inspiration came from the DMC (DJ) Battles and dancehall reggae sound clash culture, as well as the fact that there was a market being totally ignored. My cousin connected me with a skilled local DJ who goes by the name DJ Tab, as well as a then up-and-coming west end rapper named Aristo. I would later reach out to an upstart publication called *Urbanology Magazine*, that published their first issue right around the same time I began BBM. They initially came on board as sponsors and would ultimately serve as guest judges and creative support for our first beat battle on March 26, 2005.

HITTING THE STREETS

Our street team for this first battle consisted of my cousin, Curtis and me. In the coldest months of the year, January and February, we hit the pavement and stood outside clubs until the wee hours of the morning. By about 1am some people would still be entering the clubs but, some would also be making an early exit. We caught anyone moving.

We hit up every parking lot in the entertainment district and anybody who looked like they might be interested in this beat battle thing that nobody seemed familiar with. I designed the flyer myself, with limited designing experience but, with no funds to spend on a real designer. I found a picture online of someone playing an MPC drum machine, threw some text over it and that was it. I still remember one night standing outside a club on Peter Street, handing a flyer to some random Dread, who took one look at it and frisbee'd that shit like a muthafucka. That shit hurt.

I knew the flyer wasn't done professionally, but it was my event and I designed the flyer. Strangely, four years later in October 2009, at this exact same club, under a different name, we would celebrate Boi-1da's **1st annual** birthday party and all his success with the **smash hits** "Best I Ever Had" and "Forever." Funny how life works.

HITTING THE AIRWAVES – PROJECT BOUNCE

One of the most powerful forces in the city during the early stages of BBM was a late-night radio show on CIUT 89.5FM, that was called "Project Bounce", run by a guy named Nation and a crew of DJs. Continuing the legacy that began with Ron Nelson, with the Fantastic Voyage Program on CKLN 88.1 FM in the mid-80s, Project Bounce was a breath of fresh air for Toronto. This was the home of underground Hip-Hop and the place where all local artists vied for a piece of the limelight.

If artists had beef in the city, this was the ideal place for it to get aired out, before Facebook and Twitter came along. I ran some ads on this station, which I voiced myself, over a KRS One instrumental track "Outta Here", and the rest was history. We struck a chord with listeners. My experience hosting a radio show in earlier years at CKDU 88.1 FM in Halifax, in addition to winning an award, was about to pay off. I voiced it at a spot in Mississauga called Sound Resolve studios, which is one of those spots where "if the walls could talk", for all the history that took place in that studio, we would learn some incredible things.

This was a very comfortable home studio, owned by two brothers Scott and Jon. I can't remember how we initially met but, luckily we did. They helped me out in a lot of crunch situations. Whether we needed to voice an ad, figure out a prize for the battle winners, needed footage for the BBM documentary, or help setting up the stage and equipment, they seemed to be able to handle any technical problem that would arise.

THE ADVENT OF SOCIAL MEDIA

The first two social media platforms I utilized in the early days was a site called Friendster and MySpace. Currently, Friendster operates a lot different than it originally did. But, back in late 2004 to early

2005, it was a hot commodity, especially for the Asian population. I would spend most of my days just adding new friends, and then I would hit them up with a promo flyer or little bits of information on the BBM movement. I suspect a lot of the early battlers of Asian descent might have found out about BBM through this medium.

Then came MySpace, which was the hottest shit online for artists. Whether it was a newcomer rapper trying to build his fanbase or an established artist, they all had to make effective use of MySpace to stay relevant. We used it to the best of our ability to reach producers and anybody possibly connected to producers, in the music industry or not.

Facebook, Twitter, Instagram, SnapChat and all the rest were not yet in existence. YouTube came into existence at the same time as BBM, but was not nearly as common as it is today, so we didn't really take advantage of it the way people do today. The first BBM video I ever seen on YouTube was a video that Boi-1da uploaded in 2006 from his account, titled "Drake Accapella At Battle of the Beatmakers." However, I wouldn't become aware of it until a couple years later.

48 PRODUCERS TO BATTLE

The combined efforts of all our legwork in promoting this groundbreaking beat battle would attract a total of 48 producers, with 16 battling in each category. Some of the names who participated in this groundbreaking battle include:

> Bone Killa, Smokey (Smokeshop), PHS, J Staffz, Meekone, Radex, Soya Beatz, Blanxx, Da Influence, Just Shine, Shadow Skillz, Cherokee Kid, DSP, Denny Definit, Casciple Wallholder, Prizm, Riddla, Finn, JLM, Gigz, DJ Roots, Numbers, Fuknut, Boi-1da, Dub Dutch, Illistic, A.B., Buddhakutz, Loop Infinite, Felony, Gericco and Ali-K, plus more that I don't have a record of.

Since the time I began going to clubs in the late 80s, there were three primary forms of music I was accustomed to hearing DJs playing in Toronto, which was hip-hop, reggae and R&B/Ol' Skool. There were definitely other genres like calypso, soca, African, Top 40, rock, house or just straight up soul music but, three main genres served as the foundation of my club and concert experiences.

As a result of this, I implemented three different categories for producers to compete against one another, realizing that producers often have different styles. The categories were Party, Smooth and Grimy. Party category was for the producers who were accustomed to making club bangers or just something that gave you that Missy Elliot/Timberland feel or DMX "Party Up In Here" or Chingy "Right Thurr" type of feel. Smooth category was for the producers who were accustomed to making something that gave you that J Dilla "So Far To Go" or Biggie "One More Chance" or Common "The Light" type of feel. Grimy category was for the producers who were accustomed to making street bangers that gave you that Nas "New York State of Mind" or Mobb Deep "Shook Ones Pt. 2" or Smif-N-Wessun "Wontime" type of feel.

Without a doubt, the grimy category was the crowd favorite. The impact of the South hadn't fully penetrated the sound of producers from Toronto, at this point in 2005, so we were still heavily influenced by East Coast Boom Bap production, with a slice of the West Coast Gangsta sound and a few sprinkles of the Dirty South.

From day one, we faced problems with these categories, as it can definitely become subjective when determining whether a beat is smooth, yet someone else thinks it's grimy. Or, a party beat and someone else thinks it's smooth. It is not an exact science and was often the cause for indifferences among producers, judges, and the crowd. In any case, producers all brought there pre-recorded beats on a CD, and would be judged based on creativity, originality, quality and crowd response. The judges would score each beat and the producers with the highest scores would advance to the next round.

There were 3 categories and 16 producers in each one. In a tournament style, 16 producers would be chiseled down to 8, which would be chiseled down to 4, which would be chiseled down to the finalists for that category, until one producer was left standing. Unlike future battles where we would have a proper stage for the producers to stand on, for this initial battle all the producers were bunched together in the kitchen, which was directly behind the stage.

So, as we would call them out one-by-one, they would emerge from the kitchen and make their way to the DJ booth, where they would hand DJ Tab their beat CD and stand there waiting to see if the crowd was rockin' to their beats or not. Some producers were extremely nervous and others felt like they were at home. Some producers brought their whole block with them for support because it was figured that the crowd might be able to sway the judges if the response was big enough, especially if a tiebreaker was to occur. Yet, other producers either came solo or with no more than one or two people. Strangely, from what I recall, the winners for the night came with the smallest entourages. One came with a couple friends, one came with just his uncle and another came with just his girl.

BEATMAKER VS PRODUCER

Prior to the battle, I never heard of one single producer among those who registered, except Smokey who was a friend of my cousin, Curtis James. I would come to find out that some of the producers were approaching 30-years-old, while others were minors and were not supposed to even be in the venue. I didn't anticipate minors joining the battle and didn't even think twice about this situation arising. I was not really that familiar with software at the time, so most of the producers I figured would enter were those using the traditional Triton keyboards or MPC drum machines, which usually meant dudes who had money to spend, and as a result were usually above 18-years-old. I was dead wrong.

As we would ask the producers to identify the equipment they used during the application process, we would come to find out that it was fairly balanced between hardware and software users. But, we later noticed a divide between those from a hardware background feeling that they were real "producers", while considering the software users merely "beatmakers". Of course, there were many who utilized both hardware and software. But this talk about beatmakers vs. producers began to take on a life of its own.

The software at the time were programs like Cool Edit Pro, Reason, and the widely popular Fruity Loops, which would later become FL Studio, as well as various plugins and samples downloaded from various websites. Many of these software programs were "crack versions" a.k.a. not paid for. In many cases, producers who used Fruity Loops didn't get the warmest response, simply because the name alone was seen as a joke. The producers who demanded respect used equipment like Triton keyboards, MPC drum machines, Roland MVs, SP 1200s, 808s, Technic 1200 Turntables and crates of records.

So, in essence, you had producers who spent zero dollars on their production arsenal competing with producers who spent upwards of $10,000 dollars. The fact that the low investment "beatmakers" were competing and even beating the high investment "producers" in battles didn't sit well with quite a few people. I suspect the same sentiments were shared when the DJ Culture changed from Turntables to CDJ's, and from CDJ's to Controllers. Change is not always appreciated and I heard countless complaints about software producers somehow being sub-par. Over time we would come to realize that equipment alone doesn't determine your greatness. The creative genius behind the equipment does.

THE TURNOUT

The venue we used for the first battle was a spot near Dundas Street and Dixie Road in Mississauga, called the 2nd Floor Lounge. I recall the club manager showing me an email he got from California from a producer who somehow heard about the battle and wanted to participate. I didn't know what to make of it. I thought he made it up, until I seen the actual email. Did Cali even know that Toronto even existed in 2005 was debatable. Other than a Cali artist coming to perform in Toronto, it was a stretch of the imagination to think someone from the West Coast would consider travelling to Toronto to enter a beat battle in 2005.

I guess I didn't fully believe in the power of social media in those days. I sensed we were onto something with this Battle of the Beat Makers thing. I had no idea what to expect exactly when it finally went down. I did everything within my abilities to promote, market, and build a buzz about this battle. I figured I might be at a slight disadvantage because we held this first battle in Mississauga, a suburb to the west of Toronto, and I didn't see people willing to travel across the city just to hear producers play beats. I was dead wrong.

When I rolled up to the venue early to set up and get everything straight with the venue manager, there were already a few cars in the parking lot. I thought this was kinda odd, being that I showed up almost two hours before the doors were to open. I spent the next hour or so feeling out the venue, getting the stage ready, door staff ready, security ready, DJ and Host ready, judges ready. It was about this time that the venue manager gave me the head signal to come outside. I stepped outside and seen a lineup that almost wrapped around the venue. I was shocked. The venue manager said he never saw that happen before, especially for a random event that wasn't already established.

I wore a custom Maple Leaf jacket designed by my cousin and designer Curtis James, which happened to be a bright red. I didn't think nothing of it but, we were still in the midst of the Blood & Crips phenomenon that swept through Toronto in the mid-90s. I could feel the hard looks from some people who obviously travelled from various hoods in the city and most likely came from Crip blocks. One of the bigger hoods in Toronto is Rexdale, which is next door to Mississauga, so I assumed they were heavily in attendance. No violence happened that night, nor at any other BBM event, although the air always felt like something could happen at any moment. That was just a part of the culture.

BBM has always remained an event heavily attended by all the hoods. Yet, no violence. The audience was overwhelmingly from the west end and being that the host, Aristo, was heavily representing the whole west end movement, with his *West End Ryders* mixtape series, it would seem that the producers with the biggest support would be the west end producers. That theory was completely destroyed by the end of the night. We had local publications like Mississauga News to National outlets like CBC Radio in attendance. We had a lot of minors and new school hip-hop heads, but we also had an equal balance of older heads. This made the crowd reaction to beats even more interesting. Cause after hearing dozens of beats, some people became restless and numb to hearing the subpar beats. It would take a handful of producers with a special kind of ear, to almost foresee what it would take to rock the crowd.

CHAMPION SOUND

After taking out 15 other producers for their respective categories, the finalists for the first edition of Battle of the Beat Makers were: Boi-1da (Party Beat), Felony (Smooth Beat) and Gigz (Grimy Beat).

BOI-1DA

The young phenom who defied beat battle logic and didn't roll with a whole block to support him, but won the crowd over the good ol' fashion way, with raw talent. Incidentally, he put Ajax on the map and made it cool for a kid to come from suburbia and be ranked among the top producers in the city, all while just being 18 years of age.

FELONY

A master at chopping samples, Felony was a breath of fresh air when he stepped up to play his beats. He seemed like someone who had waited years for this day to come, to showcase his arsenal of hidden gems. He came with a powerful selection of beats and a stage presence that indicated he was fully prepared. Appearing on stage with a female who rocked a t-shirt saying "Produced By Felony".

GIGZ

Heavily influenced by conscious music, primarily reggae. Although also influenced by jazz and hip-hop, the backbone of his musical foundation is clearly reggae, which can be felt through the use of his heavy drums and basslines. You will hardly find a Gigz beat without a heavy dose of either of those main ingredients. Some of his beats sound like something you would beat somebody up too.

PRIZES

With a very limited budget, and at a time when Toronto producers had little to no exposure or resources to assist them with their careers, we continuously sought ways to support their growth. We compiled a few prizes such as software programs, press/publicity and connections with aspiring and established artists. Producers won studio time to get their tracks mixed and mastered, as well as, features on mixtapes, features on the Battle of the Beat Makers documentary, a full page spread in Urbanology Magazine, which quickly spread the word around town about the winning producers. And, possibly bigger than all the prizes combined, they earned Street Cred, which caused their names to be ringing around the city.

CHAPTER 3

BATTLE OF THE BEAT MAKERS

(BBM II - MAY 2005)

A NEW VENUE

With the overwhelming response we received from our recent battle, the pressure was on to keep the momentum going, so we had to move fast. I immediately began searching for a new venue but, this time it definitely had to be in the heart of Toronto so that it would be easily accessible for those who couldn't commute to Mississauga. I reached out to a downtown venue that was known as Fez Batik (129 Peter Street at Richmond Street West), which is currently a homeless shelter. After a sit down with the booking guy, we came to an agreement that I thought would work perfectly, or so I thought.

Realizing that unless you had certain connections, which we didn't have, getting an ideal venue for a Hip-Hop event was becoming more uncertain by the month, especially with the increasing violence taking place in the city at the time. So, I calculated or rather, miscalculated that we could somehow do the event from 5:00pm-10:00pm, which would then enable the booking guy to book another event after our show and make more money. As I said, without those inner connections, urban promoters often have to end up taking shitty booking arrangements just to pull a show off, even if the venue is a hole in the wall.

In this case, Fez Batik wasn't that bad aesthetically. But, since we were in a tight situation to keep the momentum going that we quickly amassed seemingly overnight, I had to offer them a deal where they couldn't lose. It was an early event, so the chances of violence were perceived to be limited and they would get to keep all the bar money from both events; our event and the one after.

A FRIEND IN NEED - NEWT

In making every effort to make this second battle live up to the hype of the first battle, I needed to make some more contacts that would help build the brand. Since we decided to add the live element to Battle of the Beat Makers, we needed a source to get the equipment from. Someone put me on to Long & McQuade, the largest supplier of DJ and musical equipment in the country. I wasn't overly familiar with them prior to reaching out to them because I really had no reason to be.

Once I became aware of the position they held for producers, who were looking for equipment, I reached out and was somehow connected to a guy named Newt. He was a seasoned Accounts Manager who seemed like he had been at Long & McQuade longer than I been alive. I wore many hats during the inception of BBM, but one that I wasn't overjoyed about was having to knock on doors and ask for sponsorships, as I was always more comfortable in just creating my own way. Go it alone, you might say. I certainly had no issues when it came to a lack of ideas or creativity, but the financial means usually presented a problem.

It sometimes felt demoralizing when you had a hot idea that you felt would work but, you have to beg people to believe in your vision. I hated it. But, dealing with Newt didn't feel like begging, it felt like trying to persuade an uncle about a good idea. In any case, I sat down with Newt and explained BBM, the idea, the response we received, the media coverage we got and what I thought we could do in the future. He listened tentatively, but it was a little hard to gauge whether it was a look of "I heard this all before" or "I think he might be onto something." Either way, the end result was I walked away with all the equipment I needed to make the battle happen. He opened me an account with Long & McQuade, so now I could rent all the equipment I ever needed. I got the keyboards, drum machines, and headphones to set up the live aspect for producers to create beats live on the spot. Sound Resolve studio provided the laptops and we were good to go. And being that the Long & McQuade store on Bloor Street in Toronto was only a short drive away from the venue, we could easily make any last-minute runs prior to the battle, which we always ended up doing, to make sure everything runs smoothly.

I would reach back out to Newt a year later and was surprised that he wouldn't return my calls or emails. To my knowledge, I didn't do anything that could jeopardize the relationship. Knowing the fickle nature of a lot of relationships in the local music "industry," it sat in the back of my mind for months as I wondered what I did that caused him not to at least return a call or reply to an email. I would later find out Newt, my initial connection to Long & McQuade had suffered a heart attack and passed away. Wow.

LIVE ON THE SPOT

Looking back over the years, it became apparent that almost every battle had something different than the previous one. We were constantly trying to innovate and raise the bar. And being that we didn't have a measuring stick to compare ourselves too, or an event that we could directly pattern ourselves after, we were basically going through trial and error, trying to figure out the terrain as we went along. This is what eventually led us to incorporating the "live" element of the battle, where producers would be sanctioned with the task of making a beat live on the spot.

During the preliminary rounds producers would still play their pre-selected beats from a CD. But, once we were down to the two finalists in each category, they would have to show and prove that they could produce a dope track live in front of the crowd. The layout of the venue made it a little difficult to present this aspect of the battle but, it was kind of a lower tier, to the side of the main floor, where a crowd of people surrounded the two finalist producers, while they had 15-minutes to produce some fire. This was also a way to ensure that producers weren't stealing beats and misrepresenting them as their own.

As our usual model has been to have the producers bring their pre-selected beats on a CD, we would often hear spectators and critics say that it would be better, or at least interesting, if the producers made the beats live on the spot. So, we gave it a try. In hindsight, there is no real entertainment in watching a producer make a beat live, especially if it's a software producer, as opposed to a hardware producer where you at least get to see them bangin' on some drum pads, chopping samples and/or messing around with a keyboard. However, as technology was changing so quickly, there was an influx of new producers who were only familiar with software.

Unfortunately, we misplaced the official list of all the producers who participated in this second edition of Battle of the Beat Makers.

JUDGEMENT DAY 2

The judges selected for this battle included: Nation (Project Bounce 89.5 FM), Gavin Sheppard (I.C. Visions/Foundation) and Wisdome/Bun-It-All (Asphalt Regime/Universal Music Canada).

NATION

Being one of the more powerful voices on the airwaves at the time and running the hottest show at the time, Project Bounce, it made sense to have him involved as a guest judge. This would serve us immensely after the fact, being that we ended up doing a battle live on the air at Project Bounce, out of necessity.

GAVIN SHEPPARD

The Remix Project didn't exist at the time, but its founder, Gavin Sheppard, was making things happen with his I.C. Visions/Foundation projects, working with young talent in the South Etobicoke area. He seemed to personally know many of the young producers at the time and had a good ear for talent. In later years, many of the producers who would enter BBM also participated in The Remix Project at some point.

WIZDOME/BUN-IT-ALL

As the Canadian wing of the largest record company in the world, we always felt it made sense to have Universal Music Canada involved with BBM. It was a way of saying to the streets that the "industry" fucks with us. Our first connection to Universal came through one of their reps known as Bun It All. He was one of the key people involved with building a street buzz for new records. He had a street team known as the Asphalt Regime. Nine times out of ten if Universal Music Canada was pushing a record, the streets would get flooded with flyers and posters, courtesy of Asphalt Regime.

INCORPORATING THE ELEMENTS OF HIP-HOP

Having experienced the elements of Hip-Hop since '82, it made sense to me to try and include as many elements as possible into the BBM movement. I made the decision to incorporate a rap performance, breakdance performance and DJ set, along with the beat battle that would feature a live-on-the-spot battle for the two finalists in each category. I quickly found out that this was more challenging than initially thought. Not only did we get off to a late start but, scattering my efforts to appeal to all the different elements took away from the focus on the producers and they ended up suffering as a result.

We had tight rap performances from artist like Cali Snipes and The Offense, a tight breakdance performance led by a female breaker and a DJ set by DJ Tab. But, squeezing all this in caused us to blow way past our scheduled time and barely ended up getting through half of the actual beat battle. We ended up getting through the Party Beat Category, which was the only category that we managed to pull off the live on the spot beat battle aspect. The two finalists for this category was Mista Magic vs. Boi-1da. They were both provided with the same exact Triton Keyboard, MPC 2000, Laptops equipped with FL Studio and the same plugins.

Both stations were identical to avoid any thoughts of producers claiming that the other producer had any advantage whatsoever. They had 15 minutes to create something live on the spot, in front of a restless crowd. Once their time was up, we burned the beats onto a CD and brought it to the DJ were they played it for the crowd. Prior to playing their beats live, Magic seemed completely confident in what he managed to create in the short 15 minutes but, I sensed a little indifference coming Boi-1da. I think a mixture of not being used to producing under such a time frame, and also the amount of distractions from the onlookers eager to see what he was gonna come up with, being that he was the only known producer of the two, and his reputation was already abuzz in the city, not to mention he was the one who taught Mista Magic how to produce—contributed to that. In any case, both producers played their beats and the judges selected Mista Magic.

We didn't have enough time to incorporate the live on the spot aspect to the Smooth Beat Category, so the two finalists Ric Notes and Gigz, just played their beats straight from a CD. I still wish I could have heard what they would have cooked up live on the spot. The judges selected Ric Notes as the winner. Unfortunately, the crowd favorite, the Grimy Beat Category was cut altogether. We had the venue booked from 5pm-10pm, and they held us exactly to that time slot, since they had another event immediately following ours. As soon as 10pm came, the lights were turned on and we were shit out of luck. I was crushed.

At this moment, for a split second I was about to say "fuck it", thinking that maybe I had bitten off more than I could chew with this beat battle stuff. After a successful launch to this whole movement two months earlier, I felt like I completely killed everything with this one miscalculated move. It wasn't a good look. We just moved the battle into the heart of downtown Toronto, in the entertainment district, with a crazy following of supporters who looked forward to hearing what kind of heat Toronto producers were bringing. And after much anticipation, a third of the producers in the battle didn't even get to play a beat. Damn. It was one of those moments where you felt like you just let the whole city down, at least as far as producers were concerned.

Personally, the only thing that took my mind away from this mishap and forced me to accept what I perceived at the time was a complete fuck up, was my 10-month-old daughter. Just the thought of her helped me get over the disappointment. I tried to play it cool but, I was crushed. I put so much energy, time, money and passion into getting this thing off the ground, only to fuck it up in one bad move. In future battles, even though I would still allow for other elements of Hip-Hop to play a role, none would ever take away from the spotlight on producers.

GRIMY BEAT CATEGORY

The opportunity to immediately keep the movement going came from Nation from the Project Bounce radio program. As a judge for the second edition of Battle of the Beat Makers, I guess it made sense to him to offer me the opportunity to bring the show on-the-air and we could at least save face and try to complete the battle. This was a great gesture and possibly the one that gave me the desire to continue on. Within a month, we would end up taking the battle live on-the-air for the Grimy Beat Category for what some dubbed "Battle of the Beat Makers 2.5", since it wasn't quite the same as the second battle which was in a venue , nor was it the third battle, which was yet to happen. It was definitely a different atmosphere having a battle live on-the-air, as opposed to being in front of a live audience but, bringing closure to the battle and keeping the vibe alive was my main objective and that mission was accomplished.

About 12:00 midnight all the producers from the Grimy Beat Category arrived at the radio station on the University of Toronto campus, to bring closure to this category, which featured producers like Junia-T, Boi-1da, Gigz, Just Shine, Synopsis, Da Influence, T-West, Anomaly, Tre and Lovechild and more. The finalists came down to Just Shine vs. Boi-1da. The judges unanimously selected Boi-1da as the winner. In these days, producers were allowed to enter more than one category.

AMERICAN PRODUCERS COMING NORTH OF THE BORDER

Although we had received an inquiry from a California producer a couple months prior, the first actual producer to fly north of the border to participate in BBM went by the name of Synopsis, from Florida. US rappers, DJs and dancers have been travelling to Toronto for the past 20 years to battle us in the various elements of Hip-Hop. Never for a beat battle. Considering the status of Toronto in 2005, as a city that was not considered to be on the international map, there was a sense of curiosity as to why a US producer would even want to come to a Toronto beat battle. The same could be said about the US artists that have been visiting and battlin' Toronto artists for the past 20 years. In any case, we acknowledge New York as the city that birthed Hip-Hop, so it was always a big deal for us to gain recognition from US Artists, specifically New York Artists.

Since the early 80s, almost 100% of the Hip-Hop pioneers that I grew up listening to were from New York, until the West Coast made their grand entrance onto the scene. When artists from New York would come to town it was like seeing super humans live in person. And right up until this day, if a flyer or poster or event has an artist from New York on it, it is usually viewed as something of substance worth checking out or at least taking a second look. New York as a brand has always been very influential and a measuring stick for almost everything that has come out of Toronto. The influence of other US cities would gradually start to filter into Toronto, places like LA, ATL, Philly, Detroit, New Orleans and other parts of the Dirty South.

This would carry over into the production realm, as the sounds coming out of these places was the foundation of the majority of the sounds I began hearing from Toronto producers. We would open registration for producers to submit beats and after a while it was like sitting back and listening to beats that you would think came straight outta New York or LA or ATL. In seeking recognition from US artists in general, we also began to mirror them production wise and other than the strong dancehall influence that has long been a part of the sound of Toronto Hip-Hop, Toronto began trying to create our own DJ Premier's, our own Dr. Dre's, our own J Dilla's, our own 9th Wonder's, our own Timbaland's, and our own Kanye's.

CHAPTER 4
BATTLE OF THE BEAT MAKERS III
(BBM III – AUGUST 2005)

END OF THE THREE CATEGORIES ERA

The third edition of Battle of the Beat Makers, which took place during August 2005, would be the final battle that consisted of the three categories format. We would move towards constantly changing, improving, and expanding in more ways than one in the upcoming years. If we found a newer, or more creative way to go about doing something, we always considered giving it a try. This is likely what caused an increasing number of producers to continue registering for a battle.

An incomplete list of the Producers who registered for this battle include:

Junia-T, A-Bomb, Ali, J-Staffz, AK Habbit, Synic, Don Spiff, Just Shine, Big Pops, T-Bagz (T-Minus), Mista Magic, Bodega, Da Influence, Synopsis, Gigz, Yung James, AK, Cment, Black Russian, Felony, Ric Notes, Boi-1da, Mac Milli (Sound Smith), All-Waze, Zaire, Y-Not (Sound Smith), Neenyo (Sound Smith), Will-Da-Beast, Fundamental, Pivotal, Tre Shaw, Freakz, Illistic, Klee Magor, Slang, Contraverse, Big Phil, Gericco, Blanxx, Don Vincent, Mr. Knia, Davenport, Miles Jones, Intel, 88 Fingaz and Shadow Warrior

88 Fingaz was another case in point of a winning producer who came to the battle with his managers, as

opposed to bringing his whole block to support him, all within a couple of days of being released from the hospital for an inflamed pancreas. He reminded me of a producer like Felony, a previous BBM winner for the Smooth Category, who brought a very clean and polished sound to the battle. You could easily tell he mixed and mastered his music, which made the judges jobs a lot easier. Oftentimes, up-and-coming producers didn't have Pro Tools or adequate programs to give their beats that polished sound, so they brought their muffled up production to the battle. In some cases, they scored a win but, going up against someone like 88 Fingaz wouldn't cut it. For his first time entering Battle of the Beat Makers, his win for the Party Beat category was almost unanimous.

THE ENTERTAINMENT LAWYER(S)

The first lawyer I dealt with that helped me incorporate Sound Supremacy was a guy named Paul Riley, who dubbed himself the "Entertainment Lawyer" or "Hip-Hop Lawyer", or something to that effect. At the time, he was definitely the only lawyer I knew who specialized in the entertainment industry, especially urban entertainment. I guess this field of law in Toronto didn't seem stable enough or funded well enough to be considered an "industry", much less have a bunch of lawyers heavily invested in it.

The next lawyer I would come across was a guy named Eb Reinberg, strangely he too dubbed himself the "Entertainment Lawyer" or "Hip-Hop Lawyer", or something to that effect. I was never sure if these two lawyers knew of each other, but I suspected they did. I never asked, just found it interesting that they were both claiming the same title. Eb is the lawyer that helped me put together the Terms and Conditions of the Registration application that producers had to sign when they registered for a battle. This primarily covered us to record the battles and produce a documentary that we would later release, which documented the origins of this beat battle phenomenon that swept through Toronto in 2005.

Eb also connected me to the owner of a new spot called Sugar Nightclub, near Duncan Street and Richmond Street, a couple blocks away from our previous venue, Fez Batik. This venue would serve as the location for the third edition of BBM. The set up inside the venue was completely awkward for our kind of event. They didn't have a stage, so it was very difficult to see which producers were playing their beat at any given time but, we needed a new home and being that I was referred by a mutual lawyer I didn't have to jump through any hoops to get the venue. We made due with the venue to keep the movement going but, we definitely would be on the hunt again for another home.

JUDGEMENT DAY 3

MARCUS KANE

In a chance meeting with my lawyer at the time, Eb Reinberg, he put me onto a successful local producer known as Marcus Kane. Although he wasn't really known for the kind of production that our producers were coming with, I decided to reach out to him. I was beginning to learn the important nature of relationships in this business, so I brought him on as a guest judge. He might have been a little out of his element but, he served as an excellent judge in his ability to critique beats of a different calibre and genre.

WIZDOME/BUN IT ALL

Other than Boi-1da, in the history of Battle of the Beat Makers, Bun It All is the only person we had judge more than once. He helped us reach a wider network of people through his position at Universal Music Canada. In addition, his team "Asphalt Regime" was working the streets heavy, when plastering the streets with promo material was still legal. Speaking of legal, we were still allowed to smoke in the clubs in those days, so the air was often filled with weed smoke. Judges were no exception. It was during this battle, that Bun It All got so high he couldn't judge anymore and had to cut out early. We found a substitute judge to fill in for him.

SEAN SAVAGE

As a popular producer, remixer and instructor, as well as our connection to bringing Centennial College on as sponsors for Battle of the Beat Makers, we had Sean Savage serve as a guest judge for this battle. He brought a real technical ear when it came to production, so this was useful when we wanted to grow beyond just being an underground movement and start reaching producers who might normally be intimidated by the nature of BBM or the perception of it just being for hard core Hip-Hop heads. Centennial College also wanted to tap into this growing surge of up and coming music producers, so the relationship was mutual to serve both our purposes. We provided the winners with a means to get some free and beneficial education in the music business, while the College was able to market directly to the market they were trying to reach.

A HIGHER LEARNING

A friend of mine, Liza, connected me to Sean Savage, an instructor at Centennial College. The school was in the process of making their inroads into the Recording Arts industry, by launching a bunch of courses that catered to aspiring music producers. Prior to this, for the most part, anybody interested in taking a course that had to do with the recording arts, usually had to go to a private school like Trebas Institute or Harris Institute or

Metalworks. I was not aware of any of the public colleges offering such courses. So, although it would obviously seem like they were helping us as a sponsor, we equally helped them to raise their profile amongst their direct market, which consisted of up-and-coming producers. At the time, we reached that market like nobody else could. As a result, we would put their logos on all our promotional material, on our website and also have them set up a table at the battle, so aspiring producers could learn other aspects of the recording arts industry. In return, they would offer the winners of each category a free course at their college.

This was unheard of at the time, being the relatively underground street movement that we were. It was rare that we would be able to take these aspiring producers and provide them with an opportunity to get a free education, where they could learn about such things as mixing, mastering, as well as, the business side of the music business, things like a Recording Contract or Publishing. I was delighted to know that we could help these producers in this way. Many of these producers were from the hood. They didn't have the means or the know-how, to learn about the business side of the industry. We also saved them the burden of dumping upwards of $10,000 into a private school, as this almost happened to me a decade earlier, so I'm sure the fees were even higher at that point.

I recall telling some notable people in the "industry" that we had Centennial College on board as a sponsor and the look of disbelief I would get spoke volumes. I had some people who came to the battle just to see if Centennial was really involved and if not, I suspect they wanted to put me on blast. The battle was upstairs in the venue, and we positioned Centennial right by the entrance, so as soon as you walked upstairs and into the venue, a Centennial rep hit you with a promotional brochure. When these "industry" people showed up, I could tell by their reaction that they were caught off guard. It was not a common thing to see a street oriented event like BBM, where some producer entourages looked like they might be packing something, involved with an established educational institution.

One of the things we didn't anticipate with the free courses from Centennial College is that they were for people who were finished high school, which meant on average at least 19 years of age. Again, I was a little baffled by the fact that not all, but many, of the producers winning the battles were all minors. These guys were still in high school. So even after winning the battle, they were not old enough to even take the college courses being offered. To my knowledge, these were time sensitive courses, so neither we nor the College anticipated that some of these producers would be so young that they needed to wait a year or two before they could take the courses.

And I could tell by the look on the winning producers faces, when I would describe and suggest which courses they could or should take at Centennial, that they didn't know the first thing about the music business, besides writing "Copyright by so and so" on their beat CDs. They just knew how to make a hot beat.

STRAIGHT GRIMY (T-MINUS AND BOI-1DA)

Battle of the Beat Makers was the entry point for the producer that would later be known as T-Minus. During his battle days he was known as T-Bagz or simply Bagz. He always came across as a very low-key guy who was more comfortable letting his music speak for him, as opposed to being the celebrity type. From day one he has been on that smooth melodic type of production. So, when he entered his first couple beat battles, naturally he registered for the smooth category. But, it wasn't a walk in the park. He faced a disappointing loss the first time he battled but, learned from that loss, brushed up on his skills and came back three months later to clean house.

It was common for producers to attend as onlookers just to study, see what the competition was like and as a result, register and come with their A game for the next battle. For BBM III, there were many standout producers at this battle in all three categories but, for this specific smooth category that Bagz was in, it boiled down to himself and one of the grimiest battle producers, Gigz, who switched lanes and decided to jump into the smooth category. They battled back and forth and had to draw a couple extra beats to satisfy the judges and crowd, as this was clearly a clash of two titans. There was a lot of mixed emotions to the battle and some felt the judges were leaning towards giving Gigz the win, but a portion of the crowd was cheering for Bagz, so after much deliberation, it was finally decided that the win went to Bagz.

I didn't know it at the time, but it was later revealed that Bagz and Boi-1da were close friends, lived in the same area in Ajax and even co-produced music together. They were a part of a collective known as "Straight Grimy", which consisted of emcees and producers. Over the years I would see how they definitely complemented each other's style. I would often end up with a bunch of beat CDs in my car after every battle, as producers would sometimes intentionally leave me their beat CDs, placing me in like an A&R role. They figured leaving their CDs with me would somehow help them.

In other cases, producers would just carelessly leave their CDs lying around somewhere, so I would drive around listening to beats by a number of producers including Bagz and Boi-1da, often with words like "copyright by Boi-1da" or "copyright by Bagz", or something to that effect usually written on the CD. At 16 or 17 years of age, if nothing else, they had at least learned the basics of trying to protect their beats, as artists were constantly hitting them up for free beats. At one point, Boi-1da's email address was "no_free_beats@hotmail.com", to try and shake off the shitload of rappers always trying to get free beats from him.

Although 1da had successfully conquered the Party Beat category in his debut battle, his forte was clearly his Grimy Beats, which he was highly regarded for around Toronto. And since Toronto was dubbed the "Screwface Capital" at the time, Grimy Beats were the order of the day. However, he would revisit his Party Beats legacy in future years once he became a Diamond selling producer. The alchemy of mixing Boi-1da's style with a smooth melodic overtone of T-Minus' style is a powerful combination that we would see fully manifest in the coming years, beginning with the smash hit "Replacement Girl" by Drake featuring Trey Songz. This is the first time the world would get a visual of the dynamic production duo, although not a formal production team, they were quickly becoming cemented in Toronto Hip-Hop history as Music Producer legends.

THE BATTLE AFTER THE BATTLE (Y-NOT VS BOI-1DA)

Aside from Boi-1da, another heavyweight producer who was known for his grimy production was Y-Not from Sound Smith productions. From what I recall, Y-Not participated in this third edition of BBM but messed up his beat selection in a round and got eliminated. Y-Not was not eliminated directly by facing Boi-1da, so they didn't actually get to go against each other during the battle. A common mistake in beat battles is to play the wrong beat at the wrong time; most of the best producers make this mistake at least once. But, being eliminated didn't sit well with Y-Not, so after the battle, which Boi-1da won for the Grimy Beat category, they decided to do a little back and forth battle for fun. Some might argue that this was the highlight of the whole night, as the grimy beat category was always the crowd favorite, so to have these two firebrands go back and forth at least 3 or 4 beats each was monumental. There was no clear winner of this spontaneous battle but, then again, it was just for fun.

I was somewhere in the back of the venue talking to people when this Boi-1da vs Y-Not battle popped off, so I didn't personally arrange for this to happen but, I clearly remember pausing midway in conversations to pay attention to the rumbling basslines and crazy crowd reactions to every single beat that both producers played. I could tell they were both trying hard to out due one another but, it didn't seem possible. For every banger that one producer dropped, it was followed up with an equal banger from the other side. During this first year of BBM, running out of beats was never a concern, unlike later years when producers would often find themselves in a situation running out of beats or playing all their hot beats early in a battle and running out of steam before they could seal the win. On this memorable night, that would not be the case for Boi-1da and Y-Not, it seemed like they could have gone on until the wee hours of the morning going back and forth. And rightfully so, because unbeknownst to them at the time, the frequency of beat battles was going to begin slowing down dramatically after this battle.

THE YEAR OF THE GUN '05

Battle of the Beat Makers was born in the year that would go on to be dubbed "The Year of the Gun" in 2005. Among the long list of shooting victims was my lil' homie, Cordell "Corky" Skinner, who would be the 2nd last shooting victim of the year, killed in Jane & Finch in December '05. He was one of the few guys from my hood that attended the first couple battles. I didn't actively promote BBM in my hood because I knew how easy that could go sour. I had plenty of examples of dudes from my block fucking up clubs, schools, parties, concerts, Block O's, Bar-BQ's, Caribana and other blocks. I didn't want any part of that destroying BBM. I had to take these precautions or else this platform that was created to serve as a springboard for up and coming Toronto producers would not have fulfilled its purpose. Although there was always an air of something poppin' off at a battle, we managed to get through our first year, with 3 battles, and not as much as a single fight.

Unfortunately, we didn't get through the year without the killings having a ripple effect on BBM. The violence in the city is often viewed as a "black youth problem." It put a damper on anything related to Hip-Hop or urban music. This played out when it came to trying to rent a venue for an event like BBM. In most cases, we would simply get turned down by a venue owner or they would place ridiculous restrictions on us. The major blow came right at the end of the year, when a 15-year old Caucasian girl named Jane Creba was gunned down in the heart of downtown Toronto on Boxing Day. The media went on a frenzy, being that she was shot in a crossfire, apparently between rival gangs.

In a city where racism is still very much alive, the killing of multiple black victims didn't have nearly as much impact as it did once this young lady was killed. As a result, event organizers like myself were forced to take the bottom of the barrel venues, in order to keep a movement like BBM alive, while many peers simply disappeared or quit promoting urban events altogether. Fortunately, I had solid supporters to help me along the way.

EAST MEETS THE WEST (MALVERN TO JANE & FINCH)

Having lived in the west end of Toronto most of my life, one of the only things that had me spend a considerable amount of time in the east end was working with Urbanology Magazine. They ran the magazine out of their neighbourhood in Malvern, which some might consider a suburb and others might consider a hood. But, coming from Jane & Finch on the complete opposite end of the city, it seemed more like a suburb to me.

I remember passing through the area once in the mid-90s, long before the magazine existed. This was around the time a couple people I knew had been involved in a botched robbery attempt, where they ended up getting shot. This was the first time I ever heard of Malvern. The location of the shooting was about a 3-minute drive from the location that would become the initial magazine headquarters on Hupfield Trail, nearly 10 years later.

I always felt good energy being in Malvern and was usually surrounded by a lot of creative types, some were photographers, videographers, writers and graphic designers. While they were all committed to building the magazine up, a few would also offer their talents towards building up Battle of the Beat Makers. I found it easier to build with these younger creative types in the east end, than with people from around my way, due to the gritty nature of the west end and issues with the law, which wasn't as conducive to creativity. This working relationship would continue for over 10 years.

For the record, BBM wouldn't have become what it was without the right hand assistance of the Urbanology Magazine crew. Primarily, Adrian and Priya but, also the extended staff and volunteers.

THE CREATION OF A DOCUMENTARY

I was inspired to document the whole creation of the Battle of the Beat Makers movement as a way to capture what I had a gut feeling about would eventually lead to something great happening for Toronto producers. The ultimate reach of the movement would go on to influence and surpass any of my wildest expectations. But, like any new movement, there are naturally going to be hiccups along the way. One of the first mishaps was having an inexperienced videographer involved, who was given the task of conducting multiple interviews with people in attendance, only problem was, he recorded everything without the volume on. I was in shock.

The opportunity to capture historical interviews with the winners of the very first beat battle, feedback from the crowd, as well as myself, and we got no volume. Luckily, one of the videographers from Urbanology Magazine captured some footage from the battle. After that experience, I sought out a video team, Claude "Quammie" and Legend (Ignite Entertainment) who would hold us down for the remaining footage that we needed for the documentary. In total, we used footage from the first three editions of Battle of the Beat Makers, which all took place during 2005. The footage consisted of interviews with BBM winners, live studio sessions, sampling demonstrations, utilization of various beat making machines, live on-the-spot beat battles, as well as the business of being a music producer. Some of the key figures highlighted or made cameos in the documentary include: Mista Magic, Ric Notes, Gigz, Saukrates, Aion Clarke (Voyce), Boi-1da, Bagz (a.k.a. T-Minus), Felony, Junia-T, Bun It All/Wizdome, Aristo, Gavin Sheppard, Sproxx, DJ Tab, Urbanology Magazine, Sound Resolve Studio, 88 Fingaz, Sinatra, Curtis James, Blake Carrington, Dope Poet Society, Project Bounce, Taboo and Just Shine.

CHAPTER 5

BATTLE OF THE BEAT MAKERS IV

(BBM IV – MARCH 2006)

TORONTO SOUND

THIS IS THE REEEE-MIX – A TRIBUTE TO J DILLA

As a growing event and movement, we were always looking for ways to innovate and keep everything fresh for aspiring producers. We came up with the idea to add a remix category to the battle. We would have 8 producers who were given the same four samples and would have to flip them. Most of the records we chose to be flipped, were old soul records from the 70s. With the recent passing of one of the greatest producers of all time, J Dilla, who succumbed to a blood disease, we decided to dedicate this category to him in his honor.

We wanted to again challenge the creativity of the producers who were used to just bringing their pre-recorded beats on a CD, just like we did when we challenged them to create a live on-the-spot beat. This time, for those who registered for the Remix Beat Category, we forced them to be creative, outside of their comfort zones. We would learn that some producers are not cut out for remixing tracks. They might be a dope producer at creating their own beats, but when it came to remaking a track, they stumbled. I found this a little strange being that Hip-Hop is largely a sample driven artwork, but apparently the times were changing and a portion of producers were opting to create their own sounds as opposed to sampling.

At this point, the battle structure was permanently set at 32 producers per battle, with 8 producers selected to participate in each category: Party, Smooth, Grimy and Remix.

An incomplete list of producers who officially participated in this fourth edition of Battle of the Beat Makers:
> Black Ghost, Illistic, EnJ, Davenport, Just Shine, Gericco, Colinout, Numbers, RP, Gigz, Ric Notes, Mac Milli (Sound Smith), Paul Castro, J Staffz, Rio, All Waze, Phili Blunt, Casciple Wallholder, T-Bagz (T-Minus) and Boi-1da.

DO WHAT YOU DO – DRAKE'S DEBUT PERFORMANCE

Up to this point I had heard a ton of bangin' Boi-1da beats but, there were only a couple songs in the early days where the chemistry fit like a glove. One in particular was a track called "East Meets West", which featured Aristo (BBM Host), Young Tony (a.k.a. Hush from OVO) and Blitz (RIP). I still love this song today. Years later I remember Boi-1da saying that this was one of his favorites too. But, there was another song that pretty much stopped me in my tracks. I believe this is the first time people began to hear 1da's production on the radio and in the clubs. The song was "Do What You Do", and the first time I heard it, I was a fan of the song.

As soon as I heard the intro drums come in, it took me back to my early Hip-Hop days when Run DMC, LL Cool J, Whodini and UTFO ran the game. It brought me right back to 1983-84 to my childhood breakdance days. I was actually stunned for a minute, trying to understand what inspired 1da to create this kind of track. Not only was he not born when this style of Hip-Hop reigned, but nobody at the time was really trying to bring it back to the 80s, production wise. Ninety five percent of the producers coming out of Toronto in 2006, were continuing the legacy that Pete Rock, DJ Premier, Alchemist, Timberland, Dr Dre, Neptunes, Just Blaze, Swizz Beats, J Dilla and RZA set in motion. And to my knowledge, none of those legendary producers were trying to tap back into the 80s production sound, at the time. Nevertheless, the track was an instant Toronto classic in my books.

I had been listening to Toronto rappers for the past 20 years but, I didn't recognize the voice I heard on the track. I came to find out it was a rapper who went by the name of Drake. An unusual name for a rapper in that day, but the artist's talent was undeniable. I asked 1da if the rapper on his beat was interested in performing the song at the upcoming battle. I also asked him if I could use the song for the documentary we were working on for BBM. He unofficially confirmed both. Anybody who got the BBM documentary DVD would have heard it as the intro music. At the time, as a producer, Boi-1da was the star on the streets of Toronto, while Drake was a TV star, but not connected to the street audience in any way known to us.

BBM was going to be Drake's debut rap performance, as he would later proclaim himself during his performance. He was coming from the TV world as an actor off Degrassi: The Next Generation. Although I had gone to Weston Collegiate Institute with a cast member named Dayo Ade a.k.a. "BLT" from the Degrassi Junior High series, I was by no means a fan of the later Degrassi series that Drake starred in. I actually never knew who he was. So, when he showed up at the door with Boi-1da and entourage I gave him the standard handshake/hug embrace but, I could tell he was just getting his feet wet coming to a street-oriented event like BBM.

He appeared cool, calm, and collected, yet I could sense his desire to get that street stamp of approval. He didn't really get a formal introduction when he hit the stage. I pretty much just handed him the mic like, "OK, let's see what you got." He started his set off with a freestyle rhyme, referencing the state of Hip-Hop in Toronto at the time. Some of the local names, places, and things he mentioned included: Apple, Jully Black, Mayhem

Morearty, Regent Park, Glenn Lewis, Saukrates, D10, JB, Project Bounce and Lil X (Dir X). Being the tough crowd that Toronto is, I'm sure he was relieved to get the love he did after the freestyle.

He then slid into "Do What You Do" and the rest was history. He ended his set with a song that featured a verse from the duo The Clipse, which was a big deal at the time, to the crowd's approval. Having a US rap group co-sign was a big deal for a Toronto artist. It would be impossible to foresee at the time that a co-sign from Drake, years down the road, would equally be a big deal for a US artist or any artist for that matter. Funny how things change.

WHEN THE DOCUMENTARY DROPPED

With a limited budget, we didn't have the resources to launch a full-fledged promotional campaign for the release of our Battle of the Beat Makers documentary DVD, so we piggybacked and released the DVD at the battle and had it playing on a video screen, on the side of the stage. So whether it was during an intermission, or during a down period where producers might be playing some wack beats, the video would keep the crowd entertained. This was always an issue for beat battles of our calibre. With 32 producers in a battle, it usually makes for a rather long night, so unless the beats are bangin' all the way through you need something to keep them interested enough to stick around until the end of a battle.

On several occasions, once a producer is eliminated from the battle, he and all his supporters vacate the premises. I say he because, up until this point, there were no female producers entering beat battles in Toronto. The first female producer to ever participate in BBM went by the name of "EnJ", which many people mistakenly called Enjoy. She now goes by "She Da God". In any case, the documentary was generally well received but, we did receive our fair share of critiques as well. One of the first critiques I heard was, "Is this a documentary on Boi-1da"? I heard this mostly from the "industry" types who felt the video was basically just about Boi-1da. I didn't see it that way. If that was the perception, it wasn't done intentionally, but he was without a doubt the producer with the biggest street buzz and the most sought after producer to come up out of Battle of the Beat Makers.

That fact was undeniable and would prove itself true tenfold over the years, so I had to just accept the criticism and let it play itself out. Other people felt that the documentary was a little too draggy. In hindsight, I think the documentary served its purpose, to document a part of history that I felt was important in the legacy of

Toronto Hip-Hop and also so nobody could later come along and distort the real story.

THE OFFERING

Sometime a little before or after Battle of the Beat Makers IV, I got a call from Click, who was an A&R for Universal Music Canada, and also the co-founder of the Stylus Awards, an event which began about two years after BBM and awarded the city's local DJs for their achievements in the industry. He and I had been talking a bit since he first attended Battle of the Beat Makers III, the previous year. As a result of witnessing the influence that BBM was having in the city for producers and the overall scene, he wanted to see if we would be interested in bringing BBM under the Stylus Awards umbrella. Most long-term events in the city are dependent on government funding. And most of us in the urban community have come to accept that funding for our events are limited at best, so if you can either pool together numerous successful events that can either secure independent funding or submit a funding application that incorporates a litany of different special events, it is a strategy that many urban event coordinators try to employ to keep their ship afloat. I was flattered that Click would consider BBM to be a part of Stylus, because they knew the ins and outs of government funding, the music business and had all the contacts to get things done.

On the other hand, we didn't know anything about the government funding that was available, the inner workings of a major record label, nor did we have all the know how in securing major sponsors but, I still didn't feel comfortable placing the brand that we built up with BBM to end up under another company's umbrella. We began on a shoestring budget, 100% out of pocket, with a vision and a lot of passion but, lacked in a lot of other areas. We were the underground. The Stylus group primarily catered to DJs and we primarily catered to Producers, so I was content knowing that we were not directly in competition with one another and could both be successful without stepping on each other's feet.

At an earlier time and while wearing his A&R hat at Universal Music Canada, Click also offered me a distribution deal for our Battle of the Beat Makers documentary DVD but, we didn't have the clearances for all the background music in the video, in order to make such a deal. Up to that point, I didn't know all the fine details around clearances, licensing, publishing or royalties. So we had to keep it on the mixtape/DVD level. But, it did serve to enforce the fact that we were onto something here with Battle of the Beat Makers, that the largest record company in the world wanted to distribute our work. At that point I figured, no matter who you are or what you do, if what you do is influential, somebody is going to come knocking on your door.

FLEMINGDON PARK

We decided on going with a new host for this battle, just to try something new. We just secured a new venue, where we would remain for three years, so we thought a new approach wouldn't hurt. And since our previous host Aristo, was heavily representing the west end, our new host JB would be able to bring some balance to the situation. JB represents Flemingdon Park, which is technically North York but, still perceived to be a part of the east end. Flemo, as it is called for short has strong roots in Toronto's early Hip-Hop scene.

As a teenager going to parties in the late 80s and early 90s, located in Jane & Finch, Jungle, Rexdale, and Regent Park; Flemo was always mentioned in this grouping of some of Toronto's original hoods that you would hear being shouted out by emcees, deejays or promoters. JB represented a part of this foundation that the younger Hip-Hop heads might not be familiar with, but with groups like The Little Rascals, The Get Loose Crew, Self Defense, GCP, Toba Chung and others, I had a level of respect for Flemo since the 80s. As a result, it felt right to incorporate JB into the mix. It took him a little while to get used to the format of hosting a beat battle but, once he became comfortable everything was cool and we fulfilled our objective of making BBM feel more balanced among the different hoods and various parts of the city.

JUDGEMENT DAY 4

CHOCLAIR

The biggest thing to happen to Canadian Hip-Hop immediately following the Dream Warriors/Michee Mee/Maestro era would definitely be credited to Choclair. He made a lot of noise with his Gold Selling debut album "Ice Cold" and began putting Toronto on the map, as far as giving the U.S. market a taste of what Toronto had to offer.

GROUCH

A veteran DJ in the city, known for his turntablism from back in the 90s, we understood the close relationship that DJs have with Producers. Most of the dopest producers in the game have all come from DJ roots. So I felt it was only right to incorporate that element into the judging. After all, it is usually the ears of a DJ that breaks records.

PEACE TO THE GODS

It was a humbling experience bringing DJ Allah Mathematics to town to be a guest judge. He was the first artist I would ever book for a show, so the whole process was a learning experience. I grew up a huge fan of Wu Tang Clan. Their place in Hip-Hop is above the clouds. I wanted to connect BBM to a piece of the greatness that was Wu Tang. I couldn't afford to book RZA, so I began researching some of the lesser known producers responsible for some of Wu Tang's biggest records. I came across Mathematics and was surprised to learn not only about the hits he produced for the group but, also the fact that he was the one responsible for designing the world renowned Wu Tang logo.

The process for booking him was very smooth. I didn't have to deal with an outrageous performance fee, no crazy rider sheet, no issues crossing the border, no entourage, no ego and even got a sneak preview into some of the hidden gems he was currently working on. He was either in the process of or just finished a documentary which focused on shining light on the veteran producers from New York that crafted that traditional boom bap sound. He was delighted to know that we had just put together a similar documentary focusing on Battle of the Beat Makers and the Toronto producers that arose from it.

When he came to town we passed through Priya's house in Malvern to show him some aspects of how the early stages of Urbanology Magazine came to be. We went to Malvern Town Centre for some junk food, McDonald's to be exact, and living up to his claim as a health conscious vegetarian he wouldn't eat as much as a French fry. We then made our way downtown to have a photoshoot with the winners of Battle of the Beat Makers IV. By this time, we had expanded the battle to four categories, having added the Remix category, so the winners were: RP (Party Beat Category), Ric Notes (Smooth Beat Category), Gigz (Grimy Beat Category) and Paul Castro (Remix Category).

For some reason, when we first picked Mathematics up from the airport en route to his hotel, he was reading an edition of Urbanology Magazine which featured BBM winners from a previous battle. He seemed stumped trying to figure out what "Boi-1da" meant. He tried to pronounce it but it didn't click until we told him what it said. Just from the spelling of the name, he seemed curious to know who this producer was and what his beats sounded like. He would get his chance in a few hours, after we hit up DJ Big Jacks and them at CKLN 88.1 FM to do some radio promo for the battle. Although Boi-1da didn't walk away a winner during this particular battle, I invited him to come partake in the photoshoot and just come kick it with Mathematics. Unfortunately, although he was interested in coming through, he was way out in Ajax and didn't have a ride to make it down.

He played a special Wu Tang set during the intermission. Now, he didn't play anything exclusive that any other DJ couldn't play but, the crowd reaction to him playing classic Wu Tang records was as though the whole clan was in the building. The highlight for me was "Brooklyn

Zoo" by Ol Dirty Bastard, perhaps my favorite Wu Tang song of all time. Rest In Power to the God ODB.

THE CITY IS MINE

In addition to the "Do What You Do" track that Boi-1da laced Drake with, the follow up joint called "The City Is Mine" had the city on fire. It also sparked some beef in the city between various artists, who felt slighted by things that really didn't have anything to do with Drake directly but, his influence was starting to be felt across the city. As a result, artists began jumping on unofficial remixes of the track and problems arose between different camps in the city. It would be a couple years before "Best I Ever Had" or "Forever" would permanently change Drake, Boi-1da and Toronto's status in the Hip-Hop game, but as far as making an impact in the city, "Do What You Do" and "The City Is Mine" got the ball rolling.

CHAPTER 6
BATTLE OF THE BEAT MAKERS V
(BBM V – AUGUST 2007)

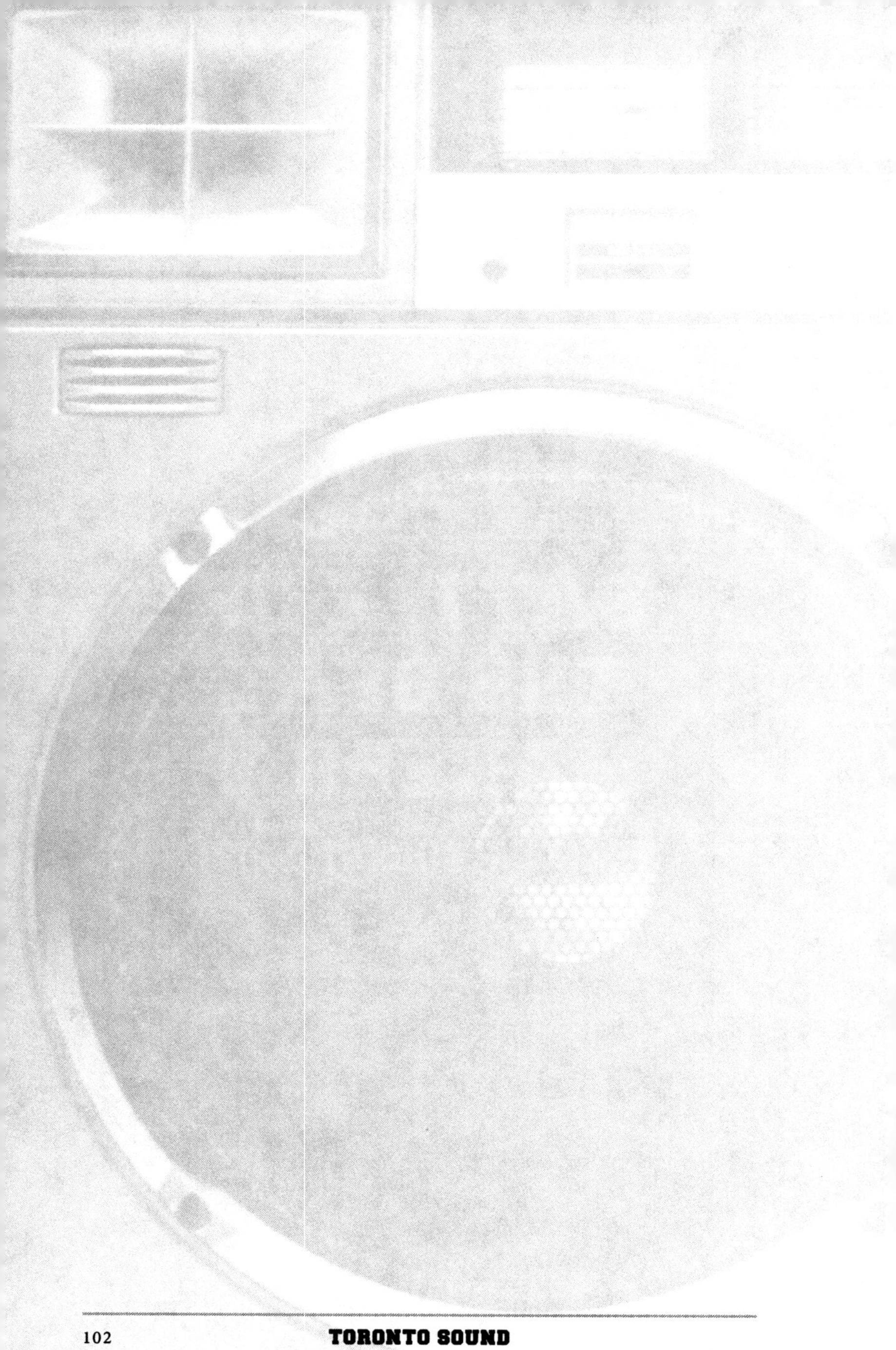

32-PRODUCER BATTLE ROYALE – RIC NOTES THE RULER

After carrying out three battles which consisted of the Party Beat, Smooth Beat and Grimy Beat categories and later adding the Remix Category, we decided to scrap the category idea all together and create a 32-producer battle royale. The new format would be a tournament style battle consisting of 5 rounds: Preliminaries (32 Producers), Eliminations (16), Quarter Finals (8), Semi Finals (4) and Finals (2). Producers would get 60 seconds to play a pre-recorded beat in each round. They would step up to the DJ Booth, standing on opposite sides of the DJ, select their beat for the round, without the option to switch beats once you give it to the DJ. Each beat is judged out of 10 points by each judge. The highest scores for each match-up advances to the next round. Judges would be looking for Quality, Originality, Initial Reaction and Crowd Response. Tie-breakers would be decided by the crowd.

From here on, it would be every man/woman for themselves. No longer would producers feel safe producing smooth beats alone or party beats alone, they would now be challenged to create beats that would appeal to a wider audience. This forced producers to take risks and step outside of their comfort zones. You might bring a grimy beat and get smashed by someone with a smooth sample laden beat. You might bring a reggae inspired beat and get smashed by a trap beat or vice versa. Anything was possible and the outcome was usually unexpected. Enter Ric Notes.

I would describe Ric Notes as the Canadian version of a J Dilla mixed with DJ Premier. He had the soulful vibe, especially when selecting samples, yet the boom bap feel that would have you boppin' your head while being serenaded with a chopped up soul sample. You could almost identify his influences before being told who they were. In addition, he is the only other producer aside from Boi-1da to ever win three battles in the BBM legacy and was probably nearly as sought after as Boi-1da at the time.

He became the first producer in Toronto to win a 32-producer battle royale, and aside from tough competition from battle vets like Gigz and heavy hitters like Mega Man, there didn't seem to be any way of stopping Ric Notes from taking the crown. And they didn't. Ric Notes walked away with software, hardware, publicity, $2,000 cash and street props for a lifetime, which later translated into song placements and a management deal.

Selected producers for the fifth edition of Battle of the Beat Makers included: Born Bazine, Big Pops, 88 Fingaz, Ill Notes, King Sampson, Amir Da Terrorist, Mista Magic, Lee Harvey, Hitman, Contejous, Jahm B,

Gericco, C4, Boi-1da, Mantis, Mega Man, Dood Staxx, 38 Special, Pro Logic, Gunna, Rugged One, Charisma, Ric Notes, Paul Castro, Anonymous Twist, Just Shine, Junia-T, J-Staffz, Gigz, Rux and Arthur McArthur

JUDGEMENT DAY 5

The following three judges were selected for the fifth installment of Battle of the Beat Makers: Click (former A&R for Universal Music Canada, Stylus Group), Pikihed (Producer for Point Blank/Tilt Rock) and Rez Digital (former Flow 93.5 FM Host).

CLICK

I had heard about Click over the years as an A&R at Universal Music Canada, and I also knew he had a rap group back in the 90s. I use to see his video on RapCity or MuchMusic, so I considered him a seasoned veteran in the game. The first time I met him was at our third battle during summer 2005, and he popped up at our fourth battle too, so I figured he had a lot of love for the movement, so why not make him a part of it. He would later go on to manage the winner of this battle, Ric Notes.

PIKIHED

I met Pikihed when we were helping his group, Point Blank, push their "Top Shottas" mixtape, a few years before BBM started. The group consistently put out hot music and I had a lot of respect for the crew. Being the producer within the crew it made sense to invite him on the judging panel. I initially wanted to get the group to perform at the battle but, they were going through their own personal stuff so it didn't happen. There was a lot of heat on the group, not to mention their neighbourhood, Regent Park, which was the first and largest housing project in Canada, was going through what many people called a gentrification process. Overall, the group had been making noise for over a decade and it was an honor to have a member on the judging panel representing Tilt Rock Records.

REZ DIGITAL

The third and final judge for the battle, Rez Digital, would be someone that I didn't have any direct contact with, so I got connected through a mutual friend. He was a popular personality on the FLOW 93.5 FM station, which at the time was the first Black owned commercial station serving the Greater Toronto Area and surrounding areas. I was a foot soldier for the station in the mid-90s before it got its license by the Canadian Radio-Television and Telecommunications Commission (CRTC) to get a spot on the airwaves. So, it made sense to me to get a personality from the station on the judging panel. He also began an online initiative called CityOnMyBack.com, which helped to promote Toronto artists, so we were moving in the same direction of trying to build our city up.

BOZACK IN THIS BITCH

We called on the party rocker himself, Mr. Bozack Morris, to hold down the hosting duties of this fifth edition of Battle of the Beat Makers. Not only a radio personality on the Backroads Radio Show, on the former CHRY 105.5 FM, but also known for rocking shows with a dope DJ known as Big Jacks, as a part of the Black Rap and Grand Groove crew. Bozack was one of those hosts that seemed like he was totally plugged in and connected to the crowd, so it fit perfect for BBM and also for the venue itself, making it a very tight and intimate setting. He knew how to keep the crowd under his control for the duration of the battle and always had a joke or two to throw in, in between rounds. As a result of his crowd control and the ease at which he handled himself on stage we invited him back to host the following battle.

BEAT SAMPLER VOL. 1

Two years after launching Battle of the Beat Makers, there was still pretty much no other outlets for up and coming producers to shine, so we decided to launch a beat sampler CD, which would feature numerous producers mostly from Toronto and a couple from other parts of the country. I hosted the CD myself and had DJ Tab mix it. It was mastered at Sound Resolve studios. As a fan of Ghostface Killah, I used a "chopped and screwed" voice style similar to the one he used during an interlude on his Supreme Clientele album. We pressed a couple hundred of these and gave them out as promo for the upcoming battle. It also served to give the producers an extra push in getting their names out there. The overwhelming majority of tracks had the traditional east coast boom bap feel but, even in 2007, there was a slight trace of the new trap sound that would soon be taking over.

Featured Producers included:
> Blanxx, Boi-1da, Incise, Big Pops, Royce Birth, DJ Cypha, Y Not (Sound Smith), Ric Notes, Felony, Synopsis, Just Shine, Bass Line, Beat Midas, Numbers, Mista Magic, R.P., Contejous, Smouse, Junia-T, Bulletz, Gericco, Synic, Paul Castro, Noe Guff, D.A., Da Influence, Black Ghost, Contraverse, David Gyebi, Wallholder, Fizo and Miles Jones. Mixed by DJ TAB.

CASH PRIZE

In an effort to continuously try to provide opportunities for producers I came up with the idea to offer cash to the prize list. However, we didn't have any cash sponsors at the time, so I had to dig in my own pocket to fork up the $2,000 cash prize. It definitely wasn't a million dollars but, it was enough to pay for a flight and ticket to a music conference or seminar, buy a new piece of software or hardware, purchase some records for sampling or take a course that could enhance their knowledge as an aspiring music producer. I just wanted to see the producers from my city win.

I knew they had talent but, they had no way to let the world know. With limited resources we did whatever we could to make the path as smooth as possible. With a low registration of $20 at the time, they definitely received a whole lot more than they were required to give. In the first couple battles, we didn't even charge a fee period. I tried to make the best out of whatever opportunities came our way. I really hoped that the winners of the battle and subsequent battles didn't take the money and spend it on some bullshit but, after all, they did the work and won the prize, so they had the right to spend it however they pleased. I was pretty sure Ric Notes as a hardware based producer, and a digging in the crates type of producer, put it to good use so I was content with that.

THE HEATWAVE

Saturday, August 25th, 2007, wasn't the first time we did a battle at El Mocambo but, this was the first time we did it during the summer months. It must have been one of the hottest weeks of that summer. One of those hot, hazy and humid weeks in the city. So, by the day of the battle it started off cloudy but, I knew it was going to rain. I just didn't expect it to rain so relentless and hard.

For an event that was about to become an annual event, it wasn't like we had a backup date. If the day is ruined by the weather or a shooting or whatever, that would be it until next year. I generally get a little anxious before a battle, trying to calculate all the possible things that can go wrong and trying to prepare for the unexpected. So, I ended up showing up to the venue a little earlier than I usually do just too mentally prepare myself for the night. Not even to do a sound check, just to psyche myself up for the battle. So, I arrived at the venue, went upstairs to the second floor where we hold the event and notice a slight drip coming from the roof. I didn't think too much of it as I figured it would either stop on its own or the venue would take care of it. That wasn't the case.

Not only were they ill-equipped to deal with the dripping for whatever reason, the dripping proceeded to get worst. Over the course of a few minutes, we ended up going from one leak to about three leaks and three separate buckets to accommodate the leaks. Thankfully, my little brother Junior rolled with me during this battle and was more than willing to climb up a ladder and try to plug the leaks in the roof, while I attended to coordinating things for the battle. I sent a few prayers up hoping this rain would stop but all that came back down was more rain. I had to make a quick run to Long & McQuade to scoop something that I needed for the night.

No matter how diligent I planned things out, there was always something that I missed or had to get at the last minute. It never fails. By the time I got back to the venue my little brother is still climbing up the ladder and moving buckets around. It had been 17 months since our last battle in March 2006, so the anticipation for this battle was sky high. I had to take a few minutes by myself to figure out how I was going to recover from this battle if it got rained out. Finally, in what appeared like a miracle to me, about 30 minutes before the doors were to open the rain ceased. The roof stopped leaking so we quickly got rid of the ladder, moved the buckets and did a super quick clean up job.

My little brother looked like he just did a 12-hour shift in a sweatshop. The host, DJ, staff and crew all began trickling in, it almost seemed magical how everything just slowly started to fall into place. Nobody had any idea what we just finished doing to get the venue ready for the battle. Things were looking grim. By the time the doors opened I was so relieved, it felt like a ton of bricks were removed from my shoulders. But, my problems weren't over. I would come to find out that the venue didn't really have a proper A/C system. So, being that this was my first time using the venue in the summer I had to no idea how hot it would get inside. We ended up having about 400 people in a 450 capacity venue, with no air conditioning for 4-5 hours in August. Damn. The best they could provide was a big fan. I still don't know how we managed to get through that battle. I can only imagine that the beats kept everybody alive, because I didn't see a single person that wasn't uncomfortable due to the heat but, we all soldiered through it.

HIPHOPCANADA.COM (HHC)

In the '05 – '08 era, the site was a key ingredient in reaching Canadian fans, supporters and haters who wanted to vent their thoughts on a recent battle that took place. It was like clockwork, immediately following a battle the forums would be flooded with threads on a particular BBM battle round. For at least 72 hours after a battle, BBM would be the most talked about thing on HHC. Somebody would comment on a particular thread, which would bump it back to the top of the forum. This would go on for days, usually with at least 5 to 8 threads of substance, some cleverly created by us and some not.

Somewhere around the time we were putting together our Battle of the Beat Makers Documentary DVD, we reached out to them. Being that they had a pretty strong following we would get some ads on their website in return for slapping their logo on our promotional material. HHC was pretty much the online version of the streets, way before the traditional "social media" existed. I'm sure we found tons of producers through HHC and tons found us.

At the time when we started, it was common to see links to songs by local artists on the front page of the HHC site. That is what they were there for, to promote Hip-Hop by Canadian artists. So, it was the norm to highlight a song by solely stating the name of the song and the artist. But over the course of several months and with the increasing popularity of BBM, I began noticing that songs were now highlighting the title, the name of the artist, and the name of the producers.

This was a turning point for Canadian Producers. They were no longer relegated to the background. They were now beginning to get the recognition they deserved. I not only think BBM had a lot to do with this shift but, these producers were beginning to live up to the hype. In many instances, the producers were starting to become the main attraction point of a track. It got to the point where you might not be familiar with an artist but, because such and such producer's name is credited, people would check for it. In terms of Toronto or Canada, HHC is the first place I noticed this change in the status and recognition of our producers, aside from us and Urbanology Magazine.

BOI-1DA VS ARTHUR MCARTHUR

I remember having a few words with Boi-1da shortly after his battle with Arthur McArthur. He was talking about something along the lines of really hoping he wins the battle because he had some bills to pay. He was apparently banking on winning the battle to get the cash prize and use it to pay some bills. Although he managed to get by McArthur in this battle, he didn't manage to make it to the finals. So, hopefully he found another way to pay those bills.

It might have been somewhere around the quarter finals and the battle coming up consisted of Boi-1da, the well-known and highly respected producer on the rise versus Arthur McArthur, representing the Mississauga based, Northern Profit production crew, which included Big Pops. However, outside of his crew and associates he was largely unknown to us or the crowd. The match-up seemed odd and a spectacle to many onlookers. 1da had the appearance of a vet who came to eat an easy prey. On the flipside, McArthur was this awkward looking white kid who danced in an uncoordinated manner to his own beats. He totally caught everybody off guard, including Boi-1da.

The thing is, producers have to give the DJ the beats they will play for that round in advance, so they can't change their selection after hearing what their opponent plays. McArthur had a slight advantage because he knew who 1da was and knew he had to play some of his hottest shit just to survive the round. 1da on the other hand was either too confident, cocky or just simply underestimated this unknown producer he was matched up against. In an attempt to save his hottest shit for the later rounds, he figured he would just play a "get me through the round" kind of beat. He barely made it. The judges scored the round a tie, to the chagrin of a portion of the crowd but, led to both producers having to battle again for that round. They got to pick another beat.

McArthur went first the last time, so 1da would go first this time. 1da played the now infamous Transformers beat, which sampled the popular 80s television show, along with a thundering bassline and drums. All I can say is the building shook. The judges looked like they were just in awe. I still remember the effect that the beat had on the crowd, the battle between 1da and McArthur was officially done after that beat. McArthur played his second beat but he had clearly lost the steam he had built up from the first beat. There was no recovering from the Transformers beat and 1da moved on to the next round.

Unfortunately for Boi-1da, this was his heaviest beat in his arsenal for the night. McArthur had totally fucked up his game plan and now he was forced to rejig his plan to try to get through the battle but, it didn't work, as he took a loss to the heavyweight, Gigz, in a later round. Nevertheless, this battle undoubtedly left such an imprint on 1da that two years later once he started to blow up, he would reach back and co-produce a track with McArthur, this banger would come to be known as "Uptown" on Drake's highly successful "So Far Gone" mixtape. This third and highly anticipated mixtape by Drake also featured production from the heavyweight Mega Man. Boi-1da and Arthur McArthur would continue to work together throughout the years.

CHAPTER 7

BATTLE OF THE BEAT MAKERS VI

(BBM VI – AUGUST 2008)

TORONTO SOUND

EL MOCAMBO

It was the top of 2006 when I first connected with Abbas who was the owner of El Mocambo, the venue which would house BBM between 2006 to 2008. It was a grimy kind of spot that fit very well with the BBM movement at the time, but because we just ended one of the most violent years in Toronto in 2005, dubbed "The Year of the Gun," getting a venue for a Hip-Hop function was slim pickings.

Abbas was a compassionate guy always doing charity events and constantly trying to get me involved with his charity work. I had no problem with that, but shit, I was already doing charity work. This BBM shit was coming completely outta pocket at the time, so building a platform for hundreds of local producers was my charity and contribution, as far as I saw it. In any case, in sitting down with Abbas to get the venue he wanted to know more about my personal life, to gauge if he wanted to take a chance and rent me the venue.

I had to describe the event as more of an R&B focused show and downplay the Hip-Hop side of things. Just describe it as more of an R&B talent show, as opposed to a Hip-Hop "Battle" and I'll be fine, I thought. Frankly, when it came to getting a venue, "Hip-Hop" meant black youth and "Battle" meant the potential for violence, and no venue owner wanted to deal with that, considering this apparent spike in gun crime the previous year.

But of all the things we discussed, the thing that struck a chord with him the most was the fact that I had a daughter and step-daughter. The youngest was just one and a half years old. It never totally dawned on me at the time why he was so touched by that but, it seemed to be the deciding factor in him taking a chance and renting me the venue. Every time he would see me, the first thing he would ask is how the girls were doing.

I suspect the notion that black males are not portrayed in society as being good fathers, or present at all, so to have a promoter who is also a black father of two daughters must have placed me in a different category in his mind, as somebody responsible and trustworthy. Whatever it was it worked and BBM might have been derailed if it wasn't for him opening up his venue to me.

For the purposes of BBM, the venue wasn't perfect but, it fit like a glove. We finally had a venue with a stage. The setup I had envisioned was beginning to take shape, as producers could finally be seen and identified with the beat that was being played. In the past, you would either struggle to see who was playing which beat or you had to ask around. Now, you could see them up close and personal and if you liked what you heard, you could easily reach out.

FIRST ROUND MATCH-UP BBM VI

In retrospect this was probably one of the most talented battles ever. When I look back and think about all the producers who registered for this battle and the success that many of them went on to achieve, it's humbling. This was also the first and only battle where we listed the names of all 32 producers on our promotional material leading up to the battle.

By this time, producers had started to gain enough recognition in the city that people would know them by name. The majority of the producers who were making noise in the city were all involved with BBM, in some form or fashion. This was the sole platform for them to gain exposure and shine.

The first round line up for BBM VI included:

Juxx	vs.	Mega Man
C4	vs.	Jahm. B
Gunna	vs.	Pro Logic
Lancecape	vs.	Mista Magic
Da Rux	vs.	Dood Staxx
Cronos	vs.	Beat Midas
Nineteen85	vs.	Paul Castro

Vega	vs.	Ill Notes
Superville	vs.	Vokab
A-Donis	vs.	J-Staffz
Big Rick	vs.	Big Pops
T-Nyce	vs.	Burd & Keyz
Double S	vs.	Frank Dukes
Dubs	vs.	38 Special
C-ment	vs.	Drae Sparks
Nyra	vs.	Abstrak Sense

*FRANK DUKES was selected in the top 32 producers to compete in this battle. However, he withdrew shortly before the battle went down.

BATTLE FOR CASH

BBM embodied the spirit of spontaneity, so if an idea presented itself that would enhance the overall experience, I was game. On this particular night, I don't believe I came to the battle with this idea in mind, but somewhere during the battle the idea came up that producers would be open to battling for cash. There was already a cash prize for the winner but, for those who either didn't make it that far or simply wanted to put their money where their mouth were, we ended up having a little spontaneous beat battle for cash.

Like anything else, when money is involved things can go sideways in an instant. I recall one of the judges for the night, Gigz saying, "fight a go bruk out". I didn't get the sense that any violence would occur, I just thought people wanted to be close to the action, so everybody was trying to get on stage. I only recall one "cash" battle actually taking place before we had to get back on track, with our regularly scheduled battle royale. Production team Burd & Keyz went up against Mad Loops. The host Bozack announced the amount that they were battling for, might have been a couple hundred dollars. Bishop Brigante jumped in on the action around this time and pretty much co-hosted this aspect of the battle. He was good at amping up the crowd. The battle itself was very close but, with a lot of female supporters on his side, yelling at the top of their lungs, Mad Loops walked away with a couple hundred dollars more than he came with.

BIG POPS

Big Pops entered his first beat battle in August 2005, at Battle of the Beat Makers III. Almost immediately he became a force to be reckoned with leaving a lasting impression on some of the other notable producers. He didn't win in his particular category for that battle, but he came back every year after that and kept learning and studying the art of beat battlin, until he finally mastered the craft and smashed the competition in Battle of the Beat Makers VI. Although Pops had to defeat 31 producers in order to become champ, the highlight of the night was him going up against another high-calibre producer known as T-Nyce. By walking around and talking to people in the crowd, you get a sense of who they think will win the battle, prior to the battle. One of the names that kept coming up was T-Nyce.

The talk swirling around was that he had produced for numerous artists from Atlanta, so by default this battle should be a walk in the park, or so his supporters thought. When it came time to battle, Pops used a little psychology to give T-Nyce the impression that he (Pops) was no competition for someone like T-Nyce, by playing a sampled skit from the late Bernie Mac (a little pop beat interlude that Mac used during his Def Comedy Jam performances), which for a second the crowd thought was Pops' actual beat that he was playing in the battle. Pops dancing to the beat further convinced the crowd that he may be serious in selecting that beat. In hearing and seeing this, it looked like T-Nyce was about to walk away with an easy win, as he just finished playing a banger to open the round, which I'm sure he felt would seal the deal. This was not to be the case, as the Bernie Mac sample ended with, "You don't understand, I ain't scared of you, motherfuckers", and then came the heavy drums and basslines that Pops was known for. Whoooaaa. It was a wrap. You would think the spirit of Bernie Mac was in the building. The crowd went bananas and even T-Nyce had to concede to an unexpected death blow. This was probably one of the best executed setups in BBM history.

Almost immediately after his win in this battle, Pops would go on to enter other beat battles in cities like Atlanta and continue his warpath of smashing producers. The only exception was a loss to another super producer from Toronto known as Rich Kidd, whom Pops ended up facing in the finals of a North By North East (NXNE) beat battle in 2009. The win could have gone either way from what I heard, but the judges awarded Rich Kidd with the win.

Big Pops' win at Battle of the Beat Makers VI would spark the end of an era. Not only did an underdog finally rise to the occasion, which was a beautiful thing in and of itself, but Toronto producers were beginning to spread their wings and make their presence felt south of the border, all starting from beat battles. This was a much different approach than their predecessors like Mantronix, Marco Polo, Moss or Dirty Swift (of Midi Mafia), who all basically relocated to New York to pursue their dreams and build from the ground up. We were witnessing a swing in the pendulum which allowed Toronto producers to remain home and still make waves around the world.

Technological changes aided this process greatly as it became the norm for producers to just email a track to an artist, instead of everyone having to be in the studio together. Granted, I personally believe the live session with the artists and producers creates a more wholistic experience, which has the potential to translate into a more cohesive creation. But, nonetheless, this new change in technology worked wonders for Toronto producers.

JUDGEMENT DAY 6 - BBM ALUMNI

By 2008, as the producer scene in Toronto was starting to tear at the seams, we didn't feel that we needed to recruit external "industry" people, as our producers were starting to become celebrities in their own right. Some were building a solid underground following, some were winning Juno awards (Canadian version of the Grammys) and some would soon be winning Grammy awards (American version of the Junos), joke. As a result, we selected 2-time BBM Champ (Gigz), 3-time BBM Champ (Ric Notes) and 3-time BBM Champ (Boi-1da) to serve as the judges. I don't think there could be three better judges at the time, as these three producers have all gone through this kind of Rites of Passage. They knew exactly what it takes to prepare and engage in a beat battle. They knew exactly what to listen for. In particular, creativity, originality, quality and last but not least, the crowd reaction. Up to this point, it was seldom that a judge would go completely against the crowd reaction. However, a peculiar situation would arise. Something that could only happen in a tight knit community, which BBM producers had become, to a degree. Gigz, Ric Notes and Boi-1da were now judging producers that some of them had battled before. Meaning, they knew their style and basically, knew their capabilities. So, when they heard something that was way over the top, it was questioned as to whether some of the lesser known producers in the battle, were receiving help from other more established producers, based on these more established maestros having somewhat of a trademark sound. Not to mention, some lesser known producers had strong relations with more established producers. We would hear things of this nature in future battles too, as people would claim to notice a sudden spike in a producer's music, seemingly overnight. The jury is still out on this one.

THE GRUDGE MATCH

A year after the infamous battle between Boi-1da vs Arthur McArthur took place, the talk of a rematch lingered in the air. There was still a group of BBM followers who wanted to see a rematch between the two super talented producers. It was a no-brainer for McArthur, being the underdog he really had nothing to lose. In the event that he lost, his name would be synonymous with that producer who gave Boi-1da a run for this money. And if he won, well, that's still up for debate. On the other hand, whether Boi-1da lost or won in the opinion of those present, I don't think there was anyone or anything about to stop him from his ascension to sit among the greatest producers of our time.

The 32 producer battle royale had just wrapped up and the crowd impatiently waited to see this grudge match go down. Boi-1da having just judged the battle was already on stage and ready to go. However, McArthur was nowhere to be found. DJ Tab and Bozack kept the crowd engaged while we tried to figure out what happened to McArthur. Apparently he had to run outside to his car to grab his beats or something, so in the meantime the crowd is thinking that this long awaited battle wasn't going to happen. About five to ten long minutes of waiting around and growing restless, the crowd started getting a little amped up as we noticed McArthur making his way to the area, literally running to the stage. For anybody who thought McArthur had gotten cold feet and decided to withdraw from the grudge match, they were sadly mistaken. He came prepared for war.

As usual, we decided on it being a best out of three battle. Both producers played their shit, that hot shit. But, I don't think 1da brought a beat as heavy as the "Transformers" beat that he played during their battle the previous year, which is what the crowd was expecting to hear. In general, he had inadvertently set a pedestal so high it would be hard for him to continuously surpass his own performance, which is what the crowd came to expect. There was also the factor that some people wanted to see the underdog win, some might have been haters and some just honestly felt McArthur played better beats. Again, the jury is still out on this one.

A couple months later they would collaborate to create "Uptown" by Drake featuring Bun B, off the "So Far Gone" mixtape.

SET IT OFF REMIX

Post-Dream Warriors/Michee Mee/Maestro and Pre-Drake/OVO, the most successful Hip-Hop artist to come out of Toronto was Kardinal Offishall. I can attest to buying his debut album "Quest For Fire: Firestarter, Vol. 1", which was actually the first CD I ever paid for by a Canadian Hip-Hop artist. Based on my own personal review I would consider it a classic. It spoke the language of Toronto in a frank, in-your-face and boastful kinda way, along with the videos which provided a portal into the visual aspects of the "T.Dot", as it was known before "The 6ix".

By the time of this battle in 2008, he was well over a decade deep with Toronto Hip-Hop (reggae laced) anthems but, nobody was prepared for a track he did called "Set It Off", which featured the legendary and by many accounts, the Greatest-Of-All-Time Hip-Hop Producer, Dr. Dre, on the remix. There was just something "larger than life" when it came to hearing Dr. Dre featured on a track. This may be in part since we waited for years for him to drop the highly anticipated "The Detox" album that was eventually scrapped. In any case, in 2008 it seemed unreal that Dr. Dre would fuck with a Canadian rapper, much less jump on his remix.

From a BBM point of view, this was a turning point. Although "Replacement Girl" by Drake featuring Trey Songz was a hot record and video, which dropped in 2007 and co-produced by Boi-1da and T-Minus, the impact of BBM producers didn't really hit home until Kardi's "Set It Off" remix dropped. At this point I really had to take a step back and evaluate the situation. Toronto was and still remains a baby industry. There really was no solid structure to develop homegrown artists, especially Hip-hop artists and more specifically a Hip-Hop producer. On a shoestring budget we basically carried this movement on our shoulders. So, to see a producer that we discovered produce a track featuring Dr. Dre, I basically felt like my job was done. This whole BBM movement started off real humble.

I just wanted to give these guys a way to gain recognition and serve as a platform. I was content with them becoming known within the Greater Toronto Area (GTA) and overjoyed to have them become established across Canada. But, with no major financial backing and infrastructure to really develop producers at the time, I really didn't believe the means existed that would help them take it to the next level on the international stage. At least, I couldn't see that far at the time. This feeling was based on the fact that it was never done before and with limited industry contacts south of the border, it didn't seem realistic.

Prior to this point, there were no Toronto-based Hip-Hop producers who came up in the manner that Boi-1da did, beat battlin'. I never asked him how he got connected with Kardi, but it was obvious that any Hip-Hop artist that was worth their weight in Toronto had to have a Boi-1da beat during the '05 – '08 era.

BEAT SAMPLER VOL. 2

After the strong buzz we received from Vol. 1 of the Beat Sampler CD, it became apparent that we had to follow up with Vol. 2. I put the word out to producers and for the most part we had no issue getting flooded with bangers. However, I did start to notice that some producers were starting to make a couple dollars from selling beats, so it became a little harder to get their hottest shit for a promo beat CD. I honestly wasn't in a position to complain. After all, I totally supported and may have been one of the main advocates for "no free beats". That was the whole purpose to provide them with the platform to springboard off and ultimately make a career out of this production shit. So, when I received polished instrumentals from lesser known producers and just a looped sample from more popular producers, I knew something was happening. They were taking their craft serious, and that was a good thing.

Featured Producers included: Petey Punch, Optik, Ric Notes, Gigz, Boi-1da, Pro Logic, Dood Staxx, Lancecape, Paul Castro, Amir Da Terrorist, Royce Birth, J Staffz, Neo Tempus, Mega Man, Gunna, 38 Special, Mantis, Beat Midas, Wonder Productions, Charisma, Beat Busta, Abstrak Sense, Da Funky Situation, Mista Magic, Big Pops, Nosa, Dubz, Ill Notes, N.V., Young, Ill Notes, Epidemik, Jahm B and Superville. Mixed by DJ TAB.

THE SHIFT

After carrying this movement on my shoulders for four years I felt like I needed a break and also like my mission for doing BBM was accomplished. I rationalized this by comparing my run with BBM, to that of the average rap artist, whose career on average roughly lasts four years, in the best of times. I figured a solid four year run which helped showcase tons of producers, build their brands, make money and establish themselves beyond the Canadian border, was a good enough reason to fall back and let them take it from there. Instead of BBM offering producers the opportunity to shine and grow, producers were now finding themselves in a position where they could return the favour. The shift was beginning.

Something about 2008-09 just felt like change was in the air. I had no idea the sounds coming out of Toronto was about to become a major wave on the world stage. I was just getting used to the notion that US artists were beginning to check for Canadian producers, and Toronto producers to be more specific. Dirty Swift, one half of the Midi Mafia production duo, who hailed from Ottawa, Ontario, may have been the first Canadian producer to make major waves in the 2000s, with the hit by 50 Cent, "21 Questions". It is hard to say if this put a spotlight on Canadian producers as a whole, or if people outside of Canada were even aware or cared that half of Midi Mafia was Canadian. In any case, other notable Canadian producers were also making noise across the border including Marco Polo and Moss.

END OF A GOLDEN ERA - 1ST ANNUAL BOI-1DA B'DAY CELEBRATION

Born a Libra like myself, Boi-1da celebrated his first celebrity birthday bash on October 16th, 2009 at Club Embassy (117 Peter Street, Toronto). I arrived early enough to catch him roll up in a limousine with a bunch of people who looked like high school friends. I was working my way into the club when someone opened the limo door, so we locked eyes for a few seconds, gave the head nod before I made my way into the club.

I actually felt slightly outta place as the crowd was considerably younger and trap music was the first thing I heard as I entered the club. Coming from the boom bap era I wasn't fully sold on trap in 2009, it would take Rick Ross' droppin' "B.M.F" in 2010 before I had a change of heart. Once inside I pretty much just chilled by the bar. I saw a lot of familiar faces and they apparently noticed mine. In a sense, it was like a BBM reunion, I noticed at least 20 producers, as well as rappers we let perform at earlier battles. I pretty much kept it cool, calm, and collected. That's my nature. I recall bumping into a dude, who began singing my praises along the lines of, "Yo, if it wasn't for you none of this would be possible," referring to the success of Boi-1da and this birthday celebration event happening.

I heard him out, gave him a pound and kept it moving. Somehow I sensed that I may have come off the wrong way, like I was too high on myself. In reality, I wasn't interested in the attention. I'm not really the type to make a big deal out of things. I love to create, but not really interested in the accolades that come with being creative. Helping producers become successful was the vision, but on the low, the success of "Best I Ever Had" and "Forever" completely blew my mind. These two hit records would catapult Drake into the stratosphere and Boi-1da would be right behind him. I really didn't know what to make of it all.

During the birthday celebration I also noticed a lot of producers giving me that look like what happened to the battle this year. Over the past two years we had been holding our annual battle during the summer months, usually August. We were now in October, so producers who were eagerly waiting for their chance to blow up like Boi-1da and really didn't have many options besides BBM, gave me that look like, "YOOO, what's going on with the battle?." In my mind, I had already divorced myself from BBM. Again, I felt my job was done.

Nobody actually asked or said anything directly to me but I could definitely read it on their faces. Toronto producers were hungry and being that many of these guys either knew 1da personally, or even battled him, they knew he came up just like them. Some might have felt like they were just as good as him or better, while others were just trying to grab at straws to get on. At this time, 1da's success was every producer involved with BBMs' success. They were a small niche underground community of producers just trying to create something out of nothing. Literally, starting from the bottom.

When 1da came in the venue, he went straight to his VIP area. I remember him standing up looking straight over to where I was standing, as if to say "why you standing over there, come hang in the VIP." I was with my lady at the time, so I just chilled were I was for a bit. A little while later I made my way over to him. I could tell he had a few drinks in him. I saw this side of him before at the last battle when some random dread in the crowd started arguing with him, while he was judging the battle and looked like he was about to start scrappin', but I motioned to him to chill as it wasn't necessary. But, in this case there was nobody arguing, it was all good vibes.

They say when a person drinks they are more likely to speak what is really on their heart. The filter is removed, so to speak. So, he began telling me how much I helped him starting out and that kinda stuff. I suspect 85% was straight from the heart, 10% was the liquor talking and the other 5% was the fact that he had a pretty young lady in his arm at the time. In any case, I heard him out and simply replied "Stay humble....you hear me? Stay humble". He was surrounded by a whole bunch of people, some were producers who had battled in BBM, some were school mates and friends, while others were probably groupies. There was a rumor swirling around the whole time leading up to the party that Drake was going to be there, but that didn't happen.

This was all really new for Toronto. We were not used to seeing artists or producers blow up right in front of our faces. This is not and never was the norm for Toronto. We have been the underdogs since the early 80s, when we used to invite DJs from the U.S. to come up and battle it out, Canada vs U.S. style. We had a few bright spots sprinkled throughout the 90s, and early 2000s, but they paled in comparison to what was starting to happen now. Nobody could have possibly prepared us for this shift. New friends, new associates, new managers, new groupies and new opportunities. The city came out to celebrate something that they never seen before, a Toronto producer who came all the way up.

Aside from catching up with 1da, almost equally as impactful was catching up with my homie Adrian, who was my right-hand man in keeping BBM going. We hadn't seen each other in a while and our communication lacked a bit since I decided that there wasn't going to be a battle for 2009. I can't remember what we said, it wasn't a long conversation, but the feeling around us when we met was memorable. It was like two masterminds coming back together again after a falling out. In our case there was no falling out, just a lack of communication.

I remember standing with a couple people and I saw him walking through the crowd with a few members from Urbanology Magazine, making their way over to me. For the people around who knew us, and remembered how we worked as a team, I could almost read their minds like, "If these guys get their shit together, it's ON." It was a fairly brief interaction but it was enough to reignite that spark. And right there and then it was decided in my mind that at some point in the near future, BBM would return.